"I think you're afraid of me."

Chris looked her in the eye and continued. "You know I'm attracted to you on a physical level."

Page laughed, though his words sent erotic thoughts running through her mind. "Oh, right—when you're not making fun of me and driving me nuts."

"That's just me doing my job. And being attracted to you on a physical level has nothing to do with making fun of you or driving you nuts. It has to do with—"

"Don't."

"See? Cold, hard fear, Page B. It's making your skin clammy, isn't it? You know damn well I'm sitting here fighting the urge to kiss you. What would you do if I did?"

"I can't imagine I'd let you get that close. If you did, I guess I'd just smack you one."

"I don't believe you. I think you'd kiss me back . . . and I think that's precisely what scares you."

Carla Neggers continues to charm and captivate her readers with her witty writing. In *A Winning Battle* Carla created a heroine who organizes people for a living. Things were quite hectic around the Neggers household while she was working on this, her fifth Temptation, and Carla says she longed at times to bring her heroine to life to sort things out.

Carla and her husband live with their daughter and son in upstate New York.

Books by Carla Neggers
CLAIM THE CROWN

HARLEQUIN TEMPTATION
108–CAPTIVATED
162–TRADE SECRETS
190–FAMILY MATTERS
208–ALL IN A NAME

Don't miss any of our special offers. Write to us at the following address for information on our newest releases.

Harlequin Reader Service
901 Fuhrmann Blvd., P.O. Box 1397, Buffalo, NY 14240
Canadian address: P.O. Box 603,
Fort Erie, Ont. L2A 5X3

A Winning Battle

CARLA NEGGERS

Harlequin Books

TORONTO • NEW YORK • LONDON
AMSTERDAM • PARIS • SYDNEY • HAMBURG
STOCKHOLM • ATHENS • TOKYO • MILAN

Published January 1989

ISBN 0-373-25336-2

1

CHRIS BATTLE LEANED as far back in his beat-up oak swivel chair as he could without tipping over and tried once more to remember where he'd put that woman's name and telephone number. He had stuck his feet up on his desk—or what passed for a desk. It was just an old library table he'd gotten at an auction sale a few years ago, big enough to hold innumerable piles of papers, folders, magazines, newspapers, books, diskettes, letters he was supposed to answer but seldom did, bills he was supposed to pay on time but seldom did, his computer, which he hated, and his grandfather's old manual typewriter, which he loved. One charitable friend had called his desk "cluttered." But who the devil cared? He knew where everything was.

Except for that blasted name and number.

For the first time since late autumn, he had the alcove window in front of his desk open a crack. In midsummer the breeze that floated in would have felt cool. In mid-March it felt blissfully warm. Carried on it were the sounds of the traffic and pedestrians five stories below on busy Beacon Street. Bostonians loved the first taste of spring. Red buds had sprouted on the still leafless trees across the street in the Public Garden, an impressive remnant of Victorian Boston with its meandering walkways, wrought-iron fences, labeled trees, fountains, lagoons, monuments and flower beds.

Chris paid dearly for his view of it. Even the last of the blackened snow of winter had melted, revealing expanses of muddy, brownish green, pounded-down grass on Boston Common and in the adjoining Public Garden. The gutters and sidewalks were gritty with the sand and salt needed so desperately just a few short weeks ago but now useless, dirty looking. But Chris hadn't packed away his parka. There'd be another storm. There always was one more, just when one couldn't stand the thought of snow.

He hadn't even an inkling of spring fever and ignored the temptations of the breeze and the view as he contemplated his ceiling. There was coffee splattered on the otherwise sparkling white plaster, from the time he'd gotten so irritated over a column he was working on that he'd just swept everything off his desk, except the computer and the typewriter—and only because one cost too much to replace, and the other was impossible to replace. Four coffee mugs had gone flying, two half-filled. He assumed one of these days he'd get around to painting over the stains. But not today.

Today—*right now*—he had to remember where he'd jotted down that woman's name and number. They'd both sounded so efficient, he recalled. A memorable name and a memorable number. Only, curse his soul, he couldn't remember them.

He squinted his dark gray eyes, thinking. One had to be methodical about this sort of thing. Now when had he first decided this woman was column material? Of course. The day before over lunch. His friend William, an advertising whiz, had told him there were such creatures as professional organizers. Apparently one had gotten hold of William's mind and office, and neither one had been the same since. "Straightened everything out," William had said, incomprehensibly pleased. "Now I don't waste time looking for things."

Chris had contended, and still did, that wasted time was a precious gift not to be messed with by outsiders. He didn't want his mind or his office messed with, either, certainly not by someone called a "professional organizer." William hadn't agreed. He maintained that knowing where things were and having an "individually designed organizational system"—Chris remembered those exact words—had eliminated frustration and increased his productivity.

"Really, Chris," he'd said, "doesn't it drive you crazy when you can't find something?"

It did. It was driving him crazy right now. But if he eliminated frustration in his life, things wouldn't bug him so much. If things didn't bug him, he'd lose his edge. If he lost his edge, he'd lose his audience, and if it was one thing a nationally syndicated columnist needed, it was an audience. Chris liked being irritable. He *needed* to be irritable. He was known as Boston's wittiest, nastiest columnist, and it was a reputation he intended to keep.

Where in hell was that number?

William hadn't had one of the woman's business cards. Chris recalled that much. But his friend had written his savior's name and number in an efficient-looking notebook she'd helped him set up. "I couldn't live without this thing," William had admitted. Of course, that was exactly Chris's point. He'd hate to think his survival depended on his keeping track of a notebook—not to mention remembering to use it.

He crossed his ankles and felt another gust of warm-ish air. So William had given him the information over lunch. Chris must have jotted it down right there at the table. Where had they been? Newbury Street. One of those healthy, chichi places that served just about everything raw. William's choice, since he'd paid. Chris had choked down a salad of unidentifiable vegetables—he'd hoped they were vegetables. Afterward he'd debated stirring up a round of boos and hisses by lighting a cigarette, just to be ornery. He hadn't smoked for two years. William had quit as well, organized right out of his pack-a-day habit.

"Matches!"

Chris swung his feet onto the floor and shot out of his chair and over to the sport coat he'd flung on the back of his couch. He checked all the pockets but, except for a couple of movie ticket stubs, a handful of change and a circular some persistent soul had handed him on the street, came up empty-handed.

No matches.

He swore, rubbing his chin. He hadn't shaved yet today, although it was midafternoon, but some of his women friends told him a two-day growth of beard looked sexy. He wasn't a tall man, and his lean, fit body was a result of no elevator in his building and a loathing of cabs, buses and subways rather than any *organized* exercise plan. His hair was dark, not just tousled looking but actually tousled, and with his straight mouth and sharp features he often looked more irritated than he was. In his profession he considered that an asset. And it hadn't hurt him any with women, either.

Now that he'd given the matter more thought, he could distinctly remember jotting down the name and number of William's organizer on the inside flap of one of the restaurant's fancy books of matches. And he'd stuffed the matches in his pocket. Dammit, he remembered doing it!

Of course.

Rain. It was March in Boston, and if today was sunny and warm, yesterday had been drizzly and cold.

Whistling victoriously, Chris ambled down to the bathroom, where he'd hung his floppy oilcloth raincoat to drip-dry. He fished among the numerous pockets and came up with an elegant book of matches. The name of the restaurant was embossed in a neat script on the outside, and on the inside in his unmistakable scrawl was the name Page B. Harrington and her Boston telephone number.

An orderly and intrepid woman was this Page Harrington, no doubt. With a name like that, what else could she be? Why not organize people for a living?

It sounded crazy to him. What a scam.

He opened the book of matches and set it next to his telephone. This was going to be fun. He couldn't hold back a wolfish grin as he dialed Ms Page B.'s number.

If all went well, she'd irritate the hell out of him.

At precisely 4:15, as planned, Page Harrington returned to her office in her modern condominium in the Four Seasons Hotel on the Tremont Street side of the Public Garden, parallel to Beacon Street. She had walked along Charles Street from the subway station and resisted the temptation to linger in front of shop windows brimming with pots of spring flowers. The daffodils she found the most enticing, and she'd felt her purposeful gait slacken as she'd spotted their lively yellow blossoms among the tulips and hyacinths in a flower shop. But even as perennials went, daffodils were impractical. She'd no sooner set them on her dining room table than they'd wilt. They were money—and time—wasted.

As it was, all her looking around and dreaming had meant she'd had to hustle through the Garden to make her condo by 4:15. There was just something about that first gust of warm spring air, and whatever it was—spring fever, a certain restlessness of spirit—Page was no more impervious to it than the rest of Boston.

She just wasn't one to give in to dangerous impulses.

She hung up her coat in the hall closet, slipped off her boots and padded in her stocking feet across the warm, neutral carpet. She was a trim woman of average height, and her proportions allowed her to fit into designer clothes without having to resort to expensive alterations. Her short reddish brown hair did exactly what she wanted it to, with virtually no fuss, because she had regular appointments to have it cut at one of the top salons on Newbury Street. Her eyes were a vibrant turquoise, although severely myopic, but she wore contact lenses. Her mouth was full and generous, which helped her not to look quite so appalled when she had to face a particularly disorganized client. She considered her eyes and her mouth her best features and applied cosmetics, using a light hand, to draw attention to them.

Her office maximized use of all available space and was done in pale neutrals, with accents of orchid—serious, but not too serious. Expertly arranged for

streamlined efficiency, her desk faced a wall to minimize the glare of sunlight on her computer screen. The
window was reserved for a small, attractive but seldom used sitting area. Most of the time she went to her
clients.

It was nice to come home to order.

As she dropped into her expensive leather chair, she
reached for the button on her answering machine to
play back her messages. But she stopped midway. There
it was again. Something didn't feel quite right, and she
couldn't pinpoint what it was. She felt . . . uncertain.
With no windows open she couldn't blame the warm
air. The view? She wasn't looking at the view, although it was a magnificent one of the Garden and
Beacon Hill. The sunlight, then. It had to be that. The
past few days had been so gloomy. She had to be over-
reacting to the pleasant weather.

She went over and drew her shades, then sat back at
her desk. That was better. She had work to do and
couldn't be bothered with odd, indescribable feelings.
But as she reached for her answering machine, there it
was again. This time she scoffed and got on with her
job.

She always checked her messages immediately upon
returning to her office. That way she could make calls
before five, if necessary, and not have to wait until
morning. She hated waiting, hated to keep her callers
waiting.

While she was out, she'd had seven calls. Six left their
names, numbers, times called and brief messages, as
she'd requested in her taped answer.

One did nothing of the kind.

Frowning, Page rewound the tape and listened once more to the deep, bored voice. "Chris Battle here. Call me when you get a chance— Naw, the hell with it. I'll catch you later."

Normally she would simply have erased such a message and not wasted time trying to figure out what it could be about. But something about the voice tapped into her inexplicable restlessness. And something about the name was familiar. Chris Battle. Did she know him? Nothing specific came to mind, but she acknowledged a series of negative vibrations as she played the message back one more time. Had she had a run-in with a Chris Battle at some point?

No, she thought, almost crying out now that she had it, but other people had had run-ins with Chris Battle—lots of them. He wrote a biweekly column for the *Boston Register* that was syndicated nationally. He was known for a cutting wit and a nasty sense of humor. From what Page had heard around town, he'd been divorced a couple of times and was one of those sexy scoundrels women fell for and later regretted having done so. She, of course, had her life under too much control for such self-defeating nonsense.

She read Chris Battle during her second cup of coffee and by seven-thirty had tossed him into the recycling pile.

But what could he possibly want with her? Well, whatever it was, she couldn't call him and ask since he hadn't left his number. If he wanted her badly enough, he'd call back.

A sudden shiver ran up her spine and caused her to straighten in her chair. Wanted her badly enough. A more matter-of-fact phrasing was in order! Yet her mind didn't ordinarily run toward double entendres. Why now?

"Quit dillydallying," she told herself sharply, and got back to work.

She finished at 6:30 and met friends for dinner at Faneuil Hall Marketplace, an area of shops and restaurants in restored waterfront market buildings. Just to spite herself, Page indulged in a pot of daffodils. They'd be dead in a matter of days, but the fifteen dollars would be well spent if they helped settle her down. But as she walked back to the hotel, she did things like look up at the stars and make a point of breathing in the fresh, incipient spring air and avoiding cracks in the sidewalk as she had as a child in games of step on a crack, break your mother's back.

Something definitely wasn't quite right in her highly organized world.

She watered her flowers and set them on a pottery plate in the middle of the contemporary off-white lacquer table in her dining room. They looked so beautiful. She sighed, feeling so full inside, and her eyes filled with tears. *Her* eyes. And over a pot of daffodils. Imagine, she thought.

Within five minutes the phone rang. She got it in the kitchen.

"You are organized, aren't you? Picked up on the second ring."

She recognized Chris Battle's voice instantly—not a good sign—and in the next instant decided not to tell him so. She wasn't one to complicate things. "Who is this?" she asked coolly, in no mood for games.

"Chris Battle. I called earlier."

"Yes, of course. What can I do for you?"

"Organize me."

She didn't like the way he said it. Not at all. Many of her clients considered themselves disorganized beyond hope. With some it was even a point of pride. *Am I in the worst mess you've seen yet, Ms Harrington?* She'd heard such queries a thousand times. People enjoyed feeling they were a challenge.

But this was different. There was a blatant note of challenge in his tone, to be sure, but also an undertone of something else—exactly what she couldn't quite put her finger on. Cynicism, perhaps, but that seemed too strong even for him, she thought, too obvious.

Amusement. That was it. Chris Battle wasn't desperate, as some clients were when they reached the point of having to call a professional organizer. Nor was he on any campaign of self-improvement for solid business or personal reasons. Nothing in his tone suggested he considered what she did important or justifiable. Apparently he thought the whole idea of getting organized a hoot. Yet he'd called, hadn't he?

"I see," she said, distant and businesslike. "If you give me your number, I'll call you back during office hours and we can talk."

"You mean you don't work all the time?"

He didn't seem to be putting a lot of effort into concealing his amusement, but Page tried not to take personal offense. From what she gathered, nothing was spared an attack from Chris Battle's irreverent wit. He went after everyone and everything, from the president of the United States to, in a recent column, yuppies who took their babies to parties that used to be reserved for adults.

But Page had her own standards of professional conduct to maintain. Although she was tempted, telling him to go to blazes would only reduce her to his level. That, of course, was precisely what he was trying to make happen, although why mystified her.

"No, as a matter of fact, I keep normal business hours," she told him. "Evenings are reserved for my spontaneous time."

"You even have when to be spontaneous organized into your schedule?" He laughed, a rich, sexy laugh that went with his rich, sexy voice. "Lady, I can't wait to see what happens when you get hold of my life. Call me anytime tomorrow. I may or may not be in."

"Do you have an answering machine?"

"I used to. Threw it out."

Why wasn't she surprised? Not at all sure she should, she took down his number. She had to be out of her mind. Spring fever. It had to be. Years of experience instructed her in no uncertain terms to tell Chris Battle to find himself another organizing consultant. She didn't have to tell him a thing: didn't have to tell him she didn't like his tone, didn't have to tell him she didn't like people calling her up like this at night and making fun of her, didn't have to tell him she did like his laugh—too damn much, in her opinion.

After the daffodils she didn't trust herself. But if the man wanted her to help him get organized, how could she rightly refuse?

"Look," he said as she was about to hang up, his number neatly printed on line two of her "calls to make" list for tomorrow. "Forget calling. I already know I want to hire you. Why don't you just come by tomorrow, say around ten?"

What appalling presumptuousness! It was all Page could do to keep herself from slamming down the phone, and the worst of it was, she didn't know why she didn't. Madness. She said steadily, "I have a previous commitment."

"Well, then, come by when you can. I'll be around."

"If you're not?"

"Try again."

Ominous, she thought. Either the man was disorganized to an unhealthy degree or just plain rude. Whichever, she should forget about trying to deal with him in any serious, professional way. But she heard herself asking for his address, saw herself writing it down, felt herself rising to the challenge. Then she checked her calendar and said, "I can meet you at four o'clock for about fifteen minutes. We'll have a chance to assess each other."

"For what?"

"You might change your mind about me, or your situation might present difficulties I'm not equipped to handle. Is four o'clock all right with you?"

"As far as I know, sure."

Page shut her eyes, trying to imagine the chaos that must be Chris Battle's life. How did the man function? "I'll see you then. Goodbye, Mr. Battle."

THE GRACIOUS BRICK BUILDING on Beacon Street, directly across the Public Garden from her condominium, surprised Page, and she stood outside for a moment admiring its clean Federal lines. That a cranky, disorganized newspaperman should live there was decidedly unexpected. Had he led her astray? Suspicious, she headed up the stairs to the stoop and went into the unlocked entry. It was four o'clock on the dot. She'd timed her walk perfectly.

A self-stick note was attached to the mailbox of one Christopher O. Battle. Telling herself she was being thorough, not nosy, Page noted the absence of any mention of a current Mrs. Battle. From what she'd experienced of the man already, she could understand why his marriages didn't last—she'd heard there'd been a few. She flicked off the note.

"Page," it read in a near-illegible scrawl, "the buzzer's out of order. Go outside and toss a pebble up to the top bay window. CB."

Toss a pebble. Just who did Mr. Christopher O. Battle think he was dealing with? She felt like that orphan boy who always wanted to play with Pollyanna, or that Nazi boy in *The Sound of Music*, tossing pebbles. She ought to leave. The smart-alecky columnist was either toying with her or was a hopeless case. In any event he was a waste of her precious time.

But she found herself tucking the note into her pocket and thumping back outside. Another attack of spring fever? She'd had coffee in the dining room with her daffodils that morning, and she'd been so busy all day she hadn't had time to indulge any moods.

The top bay window was in the attic. Naturally, Page thought. It was also a considerably smaller target than any of the others and—she counted—the fifth one up. Even if she could have aimed correctly, and playing ball had never been her forte, she couldn't find a pebble. This was *Boston*. She appalled herself by actually looking for one on the damp, wide, busy sidewalk.

All she found was a small chip of the sidewalk bricks. She looked around. The sunshine of the day before had deteriorated to cloud and drizzle more typical of March in Boston, but it was still warm, and that meant spring. And spring meant lots of pedestrians and motorists on Beacon Street, especially at four o'clock in the afternoon. Beacon was a major thoroughfare. Just up the street was the Massachusetts State House. How did that man think she was going to pitch a rock up to his window with all these people as witnesses? What if someone recognized her? What if she were arrested? What if she missed?

"What if I break someone's window?" she asked herself, half-aloud.

She heaved the brick chip. Missed by yards. Swearing at her rotten aim and her pure idiocy, she looked around quickly to see if anyone had spotted her. No one had—or simply no one cared. She craned her neck and squinted up at the attic window. What now? Just leave Battle a brisk, professional note?

Dear Mr. Battle,
Thank you for thinking of Get It Together Inc., but unfortunately I can't take you on as a client.
                                        Best wishes,
                                    Page B. Harrington

She'd be sure to sign her entire name.

She could also just leave and pretend she'd never come. But that wouldn't necessarily be in the best interest of her image.

I could find a bigger brick....

"Mr. Battle," she said, heaving a sigh, "you are *not* amusing."

"Don't tell my editors that," came his sardonic voice from behind her. "I'm paid a lot of money because people think I'm amusing."

Page stiffened and prepared herself for the worst as she turned to face her elusive would-be client. But the worst was worse than even she'd imagined: Chris Battle was no toad. It would have been easier if he were. She noticed his eyes first—slate gray and narrow, dark lashed, heavy browed, alert. Then his beard—several days' worth at least, the result, she was confident, not of the dictates of fashion but of simple neglect. But the effect hit her somewhere below her stomach. Finally she noticed the straight mouth and nose and the solid body. He had on a floppy raincoat that looked ready to take on anything from a spring shower to a monsoon. He wasn't wearing a rain hat, however, and a film of drizzle glistened on his dark hair, highlighting the streaks of gray. Chris Battle wasn't so much handsome as compelling. *Too* compelling, in Page's estimation. She'd have preferred Quasimodo.

His straight mouth smirked only slightly as he scrutinized her, taking in the rain hat, raincoat and umbrella, all in coordinating colors.

She decided to skip introductions. "Mr. Battle, when you went out, why didn't you simply remove the note from your mailbox and spare me this nonsense?"

The smirk stretched into a grin as he scanned her again, from the top of her rain hat to the toes of her boots, taking no pains to hide what he was doing. Then his slate gaze lifted back to hers. His eyes were filled with the kind of unbridled energy she'd have expected from a man of his peculiar bent in life. "If I'd taken the note," he said, "you'd have tried the buzzer, which doesn't work, and thought I wasn't home."

"But you *weren't* home."

"I was coming right back. Just had to step out to the post office. I didn't have time to waste writing more notes and figured you could keep yourself occupied while I was gone. Here, come on up."

"How long has your buzzer been out of order?"

"I don't know. Couple of weeks, I guess."

"A couple of *weeks!*"

"Sure. Actually, I haven't really missed it. You coming?"

The man needs me, she thought. But looking at him, she had to wonder. If not terribly organized, he did seem remarkably self-sufficient. *What you are, Page Harrington, is over the edge.*

She'd give him until 4:05. That would leave her enough time to get across the Garden and back to her office to check her messages at her usual 4:15. No point in sacrificing her routines to this rock-hard individual.

She smiled the businesslike smile she used all the time; it meant nothing. "Just lead the way, Mr. Battle."

As he walked past her up the steps, she saw the lines at the corners of his eyes and estimated him to be in his mid-thirties. She herself was thirty-two. She had never been married, much less divorced. In her opinion, divorces were a messy business, and she wasn't into messes.

Then why was she following this man up to his apartment?

There was no elevator. Page was relieved she had on her boots instead of a pair of heels. She noted Chris Battle's battered Rockports. So he was into walking.

He'd unbuttoned his raincoat, and from the look of his hard body she guessed he got some kind of exercise. Walking would fit his disorganized life-style.

The first three flights were nicely painted and well lit, and on the way he explained that the building had been broken up into apartments after World War II and had gone co-op just last year. He'd bought his place, he said, mostly because he hated to move.

A pack rat, no doubt, Page decided. "Have you been here long?"

"About ten years. Does it make a difference?"

"It helps for background purposes. The longer you've been someplace, the more likely you've got stuff accumulated you don't really need. Nothing like moving to force you to clean out closets. I assume you lived here with your wives?"

His foot caught as they approached the fourth-floor landing. "My what?"

"Your wives," Page repeated innocently. "Mr. Battle, if I'm to help you, you're going to have to be frank. I know you've been married before."

"Yes, but not to half the damn country. *Your wives.* How the hell many do you think I've had?"

"Two."

"Oh. And you think that's a lot?"

That's it, she thought, *I'm out of here. Battle and I are oil and water, and he's not going to waste his money hiring me—and for that, I should be grateful.*

But she heard herself say, very professionally, "I'm not presuming to make a moral judgment, Mr. Battle. And I'm sorry if I've upset you. I don't need to know about your ex-wives except as they relate to your present problems in being organized."

"Nothing's sacred, is that it?"

"If you're worried I might be indiscreet, please be assured that I respect client confidentiality."

"Right."

He sounded dubious as they mounted the final flight of stairs, not so nicely painted and not so well lit. They were, in fact, dingy.

"Sorry it's a bit dark up here," Chris Battle said, not sounding especially sorry. "There's a bulb burned out."

"Should I ask for how long?"

He grinned at her, showing even white teeth and a surprising, tantalizing dimple in his right cheek. "Years."

Page reserved comment.

"Tell me," he went on, "if you don't make moral judgments, why do I feel as if you're here to save me?"

"Save you from what?"

"I don't know. Myself, I guess."

"Mr. Battle, you were the one who called me. This was your idea. Unless you've changed your mind?"

She was hoping he had, just so she wouldn't have to tell him any professional relationship between them— any relationship at all—was doomed. But he said, "Naw," and started fishing in a pocket. He kept fishing. Page waited, stone faced. In another minute or two he produced a set of keys from some out-of-the-way pocket of his raincoat and unlocked the door.

The man was clearly hopeless.

With an embarrassed grin he pushed open the door and swung one arm in a gesture for Page to go in first. She smiled back at him, not very much, and walked past him into the apartment with some trepidation.

It could have been worse. The door opened into an entry dominated by a swamped coat tree she could tell was brass from its base, which was all that was visible. Every imaginable article of outer clothing and at least two Red Sox caps were hung there. Page liked coat trees. In the right place, with the right person, they could prove highly efficient and accessible. This was not the right place and possibly—likely—not the right person. But she kept her mouth shut as her prospective client took her coat and tossed it atop the others. Miraculously, the whole thing didn't come crashing down.

"Want the grand tour?" Chris Battle asked, observing her closely.

Well, she was here. "Why not?"

She felt as if he were testing her, but for what and why she couldn't be sure. Was he expecting her to throw up her hands in despair? What *was* he expecting? She decided it didn't matter. She'd take the "grand tour" and then get out, politely but irrevocably. Her time was being wasted, but what was done was done, and she wasn't going to fritter away more time worrying about what she couldn't change.

But as he tossed his coat over a chair, she couldn't help observing his Henley shirt and twill pants, and how both fit his taut body smoothly. No hint of disorderliness there, she noted—and didn't even bother trying to tell herself she was just doing her job. She knew herself better than that. Her gaze dropped to his thick leather belt, worn and comfortable, and she wondered if her sex life was simply crying out for some long overdue attention.

All the more reason to get out of Chris Battle's apartment fast. She'd never had sex with a client. Never even *thought* about having sex with a client. And she wasn't going to let Battle be any different.

Except obviously he already was.

She permitted him to show her around. The entry led into a large, open room that was spotlessly clean, if disorderly. Page had learned to make such distinctions. One could be clean and disorderly or dirty and orderly. A small, inefficient kitchen was at the far end of the room, separated from the living area by a big rectangular oak table stacked with mail, magazines and newspapers. The living area was an informal mixture of futon couches, shelves and high-tech entertainment systems and more or less melted into a work area.

The work area made Page shudder. How did the man get anything done! The work surface, from the looks of it an old library table, was certainly functional enough, but it and the bookshelves and single battered filing cabinet weren't nearly sufficient for the journalist's volumes of supplies and resources and...well, she thought, junk. The floor was piled with files, clippings, newspapers, magazines, typing ribbons, printer ribbons, mailbags, basketball and hockey schedules and the odd receipt. A five-foot stack of paperback books looked dangerously close to toppling over.

"Well, what do you think?" he asked beside her.

She didn't know what to think. On the one hand, the place was a disaster. On the other hand, Chris Battle was a highly successful syndicated columnist. Whatever he did and however he did it, his system seemed to work for him. She suspected there was an order to the place that he understood, however much it might elude her.

"It's . . . cozy."

"Cozy, huh?"

Another way of saying cluttered, but she didn't elaborate. She couldn't have if she'd wanted to. She'd just had another attack of the indefinable restlessness, the full feeling of free-floating emotion, only this time not prompted by pots of daffodils but by the huskiness of a man's voice. *This* man's voice. Turning to him, she saw him studying her through his narrowed slate eyes. His expression was unreadable. She felt her mouth grow dry and looked away quickly. What in the name of heaven was wrong with her?

She shoved aside her confusion and focused on the matter at hand. Christopher O. Battle obviously had no desire to change his work or living habits. Given his apparent self-satisfaction and success, he might not have any need to change, either. And that left her with one big question: why did he want to hire a professional organizing consultant?

More succinctly, why was she here?

Oh, you ass . . .

The answer had been right under her nose from the beginning, and she'd been too preoccupied with daffodils and odd stirrings and her own damn self-satisfaction even to see it. She had a tendency to believe in what she did and forgot there were those who didn't.

The Christopher O. Battles of the world.

Not all of them wrote biweekly columns that were syndicated in dozens of newspapers across the country. But he did.

And in one of them the sneaky rat was going to debunk her.

2

CHRIS HAD the uneasy feeling that Page B. Harrington, president of Get It Together Inc. and the woman who was going to organize his life, was on to him. After touring his apartment she'd accepted his offer of refreshments with manufactured grace. Now, as he made coffee, he sensed her beautiful turquoise eyes scrutinizing him as closely as they'd scrutinized every square inch of his apartment. She was slim and trim and as slickly put together as he'd expected with her color-coordinated rain gear and tidy haircut. But he hadn't expected the uncontrollable spray of freckles across her nose and the passion hiding behind the deep-colored eyes and the general air of restlessness she seemed unable to control.

He hadn't, in short, expected to find the woman attractive.

Nor had he expected the energetic dynamo to see through his machinations with such annoying alacrity. Had he overdone things? His buzzer worked, of course, and he seldom lost his keys. She hadn't liked the looks of his coat tree, but that wasn't part of his plot and just too damn bad. It came in handy right where it was.

The coat tree stayed.

As for his office . . . well, *no* one touched his office. He liked the feeling he was a starving writer working his fingers to the bone in some garret. Helped him keep his edge. It was why he'd chosen an attic apartment, even if it was on prestigious Beacon Hill and had a coveted view of the Garden. But except for the damn computer, nothing in his office was expensive. He could have afforded shelves and designer-quality furniture if he'd wanted them. The fact was, he didn't. Ms Page B. Harrington could find fault with the staged broken buzzer and the lost keys and could even comment on the coat tree, but she'd better not start talking about his office.

Why was he getting so bent out of shape? he asked himself. The woman hadn't said a word, and when she did, what difference did it make? She was his target. He *wanted* her to bug him with demands and advice. Do this. Change that. That was the whole point of having her up here.

He gave her coffee and wished she'd stop looking at him that way, as if she wanted to dump the entire contents of her mug on his head. He hoped such an act violated her obviously strong code of professionalism, not to mention her squeamishness about messes. The lady definitely had her suspicions. He smiled innocently—and for him that took some doing—but she didn't smile back.

"You take milk?" he asked, hoping to get her to say something.

She nodded, not taking her eyes off him and not, as far as he could tell, enjoying what she saw. Didn't he look any more innocent than he sounded? To his chagrin, he noticed she had a decidedly kissable mouth.

He tried not to make too big a deal about not being able to find the cream pitcher, which he couldn't, but that was only because he drank his coffee black. And he wasn't one for coffee klatches. Dammit, he'd found a mug for her right off, hadn't he?

"You can pour the milk straight from the carton," she said in that cool, organized voice. "I don't mind."

"Aha, there's the scoundrel!"

He plucked a little white pitcher from the back of the cupboard above the refrigerator, rinsed out the dust, filled it with milk and handed it to her. She added maybe three drops to her coffee. All that effort for a spit of milk. He almost tossed her out right then and there. But he filled his mug and took a seat at the end of the table. If she wanted to dump coffee on his head, she'd have to get up first, and that would give him enough time to scoot out of the way.

One obviously had to remain alert when in the same room as Page B. Harrington.

"Well," he said, "what do you think?"

She held her mug close to her chest and tilted her head back slightly as she gave him yet another once-over. He felt a bit like a gorilla in a zoo. She certainly looked at him as if she thought he might start beating his chest at any moment. He supposed he did have a reputation, not entirely undeserved, but he generally found people's preconceptions about him amusing, and even, given his profession, cultivated a certain amount of animosity. Controversy stirred up interest.

But two wives? What an outrage. He'd only been married once and that, mercifully, a long time ago. He hadn't seen Alysson in years, thank God. She'd married a wealthy Southern Californian type who could keep her in furs and a yacht since she'd never wanted to go out and earn her own, despite her excellent education. Alysson had grown up in the same upper-class social circle he had, and they'd both figured that ought to make them more compatible. They'd been stupid and young, he now realized. He'd never shared her zest for consumer goods. While they were still married, he'd done a biting, satirical column on the new consumerism, never thinking Alysson would recognize herself in his description of the modern shopper. But she wasn't dumb, and she hadn't been amused. Lots of other people were, however, and that one column had launched his career, if also the end of his and Alysson's marriage. They'd filed for divorce a month later, and Chris had found his Beacon Hill attic. Money had never been one of his problems, but he still had no patience with people who judged themselves and others by what they owned. He just took people as they came.

Which Page B. Harrington, to be sure, did not. Change was her specialty. She made *money* changing people.

Still, he hadn't seen the need to correct her mistake about his wives. Two sounded sloppier than one.

"So where do we begin?" he asked when she didn't answer his first question.

She set down her mug with a little thump and dusted her palms together, like Dracula getting ready to suck blood. "You mean where do *I* begin, Mr. Battle," she said with a maniacal, bloodthirsty look. "You see, I'm here to organize your life for you. Obviously that's something you are totally incapable of doing for yourself. Therefore, I suggest you leave everything to me. In two days—three days tops—I can have your entire life running smoothly. Your apartment will be in order, your finances will be set up to suit your income and your needs as determined by me, and your time will be managed in ways so efficient you can't even imagine what they are."

He just stared at her, his tongue in one cheek.

She took a breath and finished. "With me here, Mr. Battle, you no longer have to worry about a thing. You're absolutely right. I *can* save you."

"You're getting red in the face, Ms Harrington."

"Good."

"How long have you known?"

"Not long enough." She grabbed her tidy handbag and jumped to her feet. "How dare you waste my time and insult me with this charade? You can make fun out of what I do in one of your columns all you want. I believe in free speech. But you'll do it without my help. Thank you for the coffee, and good afternoon."

She pounded out into the hall. Chris debated just swallowing his mortification and letting her steam right out the door, she was so hot. He'd been chewed out lots of times, but never for being as big a jackass as he'd just been.

Hey, he thought, *you were just doing your job.*

Well, true. But he didn't blame her for not liking it.

He got up and followed her into the entry, where she was picking through a heap of coats and sweaters from the collapsed coat tree. He spotted her umbrella and picked it up. She snatched it out of his hand.

"How did you know?" he asked nonchalantly.

Her hair flew into her face—more or less. It was so neat it didn't have much of a chance. "To do what I do," she said, her breathing and her anger and everything else about her under control, "I have to be able to read people. And you, Mr. Battle, aren't the sort of man who'd lose the key to his own front door."

"Too obvious?"

"Much."

"But you think you could organize my life for me?"

"Don't you ever quit?"

He grinned. "No."

"Mr. Battle, I've never met anyone so shameless."

"Bad, huh? Call me 'Chris,' okay? What do folks call you?"

"My friends call me 'Page.'"

"But I can keep calling you 'Ms Harrington,' is that it?"

"That's it exactly."

"You're turning down the job?"

"Yes. And for your information, I can't organize your life for you. What I could do, if I so chose, which, I might add, is beyond the realm of possibility, is to help you organize your *own* life according to your *own* needs and priorities—not mine."

"For how much?"

"Not," she said, tucking her umbrella under her arm, "for anything you could even *think* to offer me."

That sounded curiously like a challenge to Chris, and he watched with new interest as she stormed out of his apartment and, she no doubt assumed, out of his life.

He went to his alcove window and stood in front of his desk as he watched her trim, color-coordinated figure march across the street into the Public Garden. But her gait slowed, and he spotted her—right there in front of his very eyes—tug off her rain hat, close up her umbrella and look up at the sky as the cold drizzle hit her in the face. A kid on a Big Wheel nearly took her out at the ankles.

Did she guess he was watching and was purposely defying his stereotype of her? Page B. Harrington catching raindrops on her tongue. It defied belief.

When her figure faded into the distance, Chris seated himself at his desk. He tilted his chair back and put up his feet, and he thought, *Page B., you and I are just getting started.*

CHRIS BATTLE WAS on Page's answering machine again at 4:15 the next afternoon. "I'll pay you twice your normal rate," his deep, amused voice said, and she noted he hadn't bothered to identify himself. Thought he was memorable, did he?

She took great pleasure in erasing him.

After making a few calls, she finished early and headed to the hotel's rooftop spa, where she changed into sweats in the elegant dressing room and worked out on the various exercise machines. It felt good to sweat. She could feel some of that strange, unfocused energy that still bothered her channeling itself into pushing her muscles and cardiovascular system to their limits. Better than having it make her do crazy things. She'd bought another pot of daffodils on her way back that afternoon from her office. The ones in her dining room were already beginning to show signs of wilting. What a waste. But still, she enjoyed them.

She climbed into the pool, suspending herself for a moment to let the cool water soothe her. She'd had a frustrating day. Her present client was a small non-profit organization dedicated to improving the lot of children. Instead of moving to a larger space, which would cost more in the long run, they'd opted to find ways to use what space they had in their Cambridge

offices more efficiently, that is to say hire Get It Together Inc. Though she wasn't a miracle worker, Page
had taken them on as clients because she believed in
what they were doing. She'd even cut her rates for them.

*Maybe I should take Battle on and charge him triple
to make up the difference.*

Spring fever definitely had gotten a tight trip on her
faculties. She had to be suffering something to enter-
tain such a notion!

As nice as they were, her clients did present a challenge, both in terms of the physical layout of their offices and in the way they wanted to work. They were
determined to use space and time more efficiently, but
without compromising their values. She in turn was
determined to help them find ways to do so.

But they were an exhausting group of people.

Feeling both refreshed and well exercised, she finished her laps and climbed out of the pool, immediately wrapping herself in her towel. She'd taken out her
contact lenses earlier and was fumbling for her glasses
when she noticed a blurred figure at one of the tables at
the end of the pool. It was obviously male. Aside from
an unobtrusive attendant, they were the only ones in
the pool area. Page felt a twinge of self-consciousness;
her body was thoroughly winterized, which meant pale
skin with a tendency to be too dry. But who was looking? She dried her face and put on her glasses.

The blurred figure became crystal clear, and he was
definitely looking. Taking a deep breath, Page steadied herself and secured the towel under her arms.

Chris Battle sipped coffee and looked very relaxed
in his skimpy swimming trunks as he watched her. Even
through the spots on her lenses she could make out

every inch of his taut, nearly naked, utterly masculine figure. There was nothing sloppy about the firm abdomen, the strong shoulders and thick, muscular legs. Her stomach fluttered without her conscious say-so as her mind conjured up the feel of his hairy legs brushing against her smooth ones.

Control yourself, she thought.

She marveled at the monumental insolence of the man. Just what did he think he was doing here?

No, you don't want to know.

What she wanted was a larger towel. Hers came to the middle of her own softly muscled, less-than-thick thighs. Even though her swimsuit was a functional tank variety, black and not particularly sexy, in her opinion any suit made after 1920 would have been too skimpy with Chris Battle's slate eyes on it. On *her*, to be more precise.

She decided she would simply have to ignore him.

Unfortunately, he hadn't decided to ignore her. "Hello, there," he called.

Page acknowledged his presence with a curt nod. There was no way to avoid him. To get to the dressing room she would have to walk directly past him. She was hungry and had had more than enough exercise for one afternoon, but still she considered doing another thirty laps. He might give up and be gone by the time she climbed out of the pool. Then again, he might just sit right where he was, and all she'd be was more tired. Battle didn't seem the sort of man who'd just give up on something he wanted and go.

Something he wanted . . .

There was that dangerous wording again. She really would have to watch herself.

She pushed her glasses high up on her nose and marched.

"Glad to see I was right about one thing," he said as she started past him. She darted a look at him, not meaning to, and it was just enough to egg him on. "I didn't think you'd go for bikinis."

That stopped her dead. Her skin suddenly felt prickly and sensitive, and she could feel cool water dribble down the back of her neck, like a man's fingertips. But she didn't let Battle know what his words, his husky voice, had done to her. She narrowed her eyes at him and pretended she had on a brass-tacks business suit.

It wasn't easy. It wasn't even easy to remind herself she was wearing *something*, if only a swimsuit and a towel. With those probing, insolent eyes on her she felt entirely naked. She could feel her nipples popping up against the thin material of her swimsuit and was glad, indeed, for the towel. Battle had less on but seemed not the least ill at ease. She envied him his nonchalance *and* his tan. Naturally he wouldn't have to tough out an entire New England winter. Where had he gotten his tan— Key West, Jamaica? *There's nothing a New Englander hates more*, she thought, *than someone who escapes winter for a week and comes back and shows off his tan.* She reminded herself that there was no such thing as a healthy tan, anyway.

"What are you doing here?" she demanded.

"Relaxing. You?"

"Liar. You're here because of me."

"Am I? My, my, what an ego. Actually, I had no idea you did laps at this hour. Kind of early for you hardworking, organized types, isn't it? I just felt like a swim."

"You have hotel privileges?"

"That's the general custom when you shell out as much money as I did for a room."

"You're *staying* here? But you live practically within spitting distance. I can *see* your building from the window."

"No pool in my building."

"You'll do anything for one of your tacky little columns, won't you?"

He shrugged, the browned muscles in his shoulders tightening with his slight movement. "I like to get away from my apartment since I both live and work there. Gets isolating."

"Hogwash. I'll bet the paper's footing your bill."

Propping his feet up on another chair, he leaned back and folded his hands on his flat middle. Page averted her eyes from the mat of dark hair on his chest that narrowed and trailed off into his swimsuit.

"I like you in glasses," he said. "But I must admit I didn't expect the pink frames. A touch of whimsy, huh? Still, I'm glad to see you really do have turquoise eyes and they weren't some trick of colored contact lenses."

In there somewhere, she thought, was a compliment . . . maybe. But she didn't care if there was. "I wouldn't spend money on such nonsense. What you see is what you get. Now—"

"Indeed."

It was the wrong thing for her to have said, and she knew it instantly. But there was no taking it back. She tried not to react as he gave her an unreadable half smile and a head-to-toe-and-back-again look, his slate eyes half-open but very, very alert. No matter her resolve, Page felt herself growing hot all over and compounded her mistake by resecuring her towel around her. That only telegraphed to Battle her awkwardness.

He grinned. "Hard to be businesslike and efficient in just a towel and swimsuit, isn't it?"

"You're insulting, Mr. Battle, and I find your conduct inexcusable."

"Hey, I was just commiserating. I'm not exactly dressed, either, in case you haven't noticed."

"You know damn well I've noticed! No, don't say a word. I'm leaving. I don't want to talk to you. I just want you to disappear."

Before he could reply, she dashed off to the dressing room. What despicable tactics! Harassment was the only word for what he was doing to her. If he *dared* make her the butt of one of his satirical columns, she'd be in his boss's office before he could enjoy his last laugh. She'd expose his methods. She'd threaten to sue. He'd be drummed out of a job and—

And who did she think she was kidding? He'd just use her outrage as material for another column. Her best tactic—her only *sensible* tactic—was to refuse to have anything more to do with him. Simply ignore him, like the playground bully.

Dry and dressed, Page emerged from the dressing room feeling calmer and in more control. Her nemesis had removed himself from his table and was doing laps. She didn't mean to linger but couldn't help it. His compact, browned body was something to watch as it slid through the water. The man might be out to get her, but there was no question that he was sexy. She felt that fullness again, the uncontrollable feeling of wanting, wanting, wanting and not knowing what it was she wanted. It was damn odd! She'd always been so goal oriented, knowing precisely what she wanted and how she was going to get it.

But all she needed was for him to catch her staring. She tore her gaze away and left quickly, glancing back only twice. *What* was wrong with her? She couldn't deal with Battle on his terms. It had to be on her own terms.

Better yet, she thought, *don't deal with him at all.*

THE SWIM DIDN'T HELP, and neither did the cold shower afterward. Chris knew what would help, but there was no point in even considering *that*. A few hours in bed with Page B. Harrington? Ms Organizer herself? She probably had a routine to making love. First you do this, then this, then—

Don't torture yourself, he muttered, returning to his elegant room.

He flipped on a light and collapsed on the bed, contemplating the ceiling. He seemed to have discovered in himself a previously undetected masochistic streak. He'd actually sat there watching the woman do her laps, observing the grace with which her legs moved through the water, the sway of her firm buttocks with each of her strokes, how her steady, controlled movements conserved energy. How her swimsuit clung to her high round breasts and flat stomach and hips. Her well-muscled legs had seemed so long, and as she'd climbed from the pool, Chris had imagined them wrapped around him as she cried out in ecstasy.

Even when she'd marched over to him, doing her damnedest to ignore him, he'd noted how her glasses drifted down her nose, making her look just a pinch less organized. He'd liked the effect.

Her cool looks and biting comments he supposed he deserved—had even, he admitted, gone looking for. The woman gave as good as she got. But none of that mattered. Madman that he was, he still couldn't get out of his mind the possibility of having sex with her. *Lots* of sex.

Obviously it was time to cut his losses and make a regal exit.

But instead, he got up out of bed and put on a dark gray wool suit that was bound to knock the socks off a no-nonsense woman like Page Harrington. He added a red tie; red ties were mean. Hell, he'd slay the woman. Find out what she was made of. That was the point of this column, wasn't it? What makes people want to organize other people?

Go find yourself another organizer, my man.

His common sense talking. Since when did he listen to common sense? His research suggested Page Harrington was one of Boston's best professional organizers and in high demand, but even if it didn't, she was it. His organizer. He was going to find out what made the woman tick.

Dressed and as knock-'em-dead handsome as he'd ever be, Chris sat on the edge of the bed in his room overlooking the Public Garden and dialed Page B.'s number, which by now he'd memorized. It was easier than keeping track of the matchbook. And, blast the woman, the paper wasn't footing the bill for this little side trip. He was.

Anything, he thought, for a column.

She picked up the receiver on the second ring. "Hello?"

"Hi, it's me." He knew she'd recognize his voice; from the note of foreboding he heard in hers, he suspected she'd guessed who it was before she'd even answered. "How would you like to have dinner with me tonight? On me, of course."

"Ha!"

"You're frank, aren't you? Look, you wouldn't want me to have to eat in a fancy hotel all by myself."

"I don't care what you do or where you do it, Mr. Battle."

"Not that 'Mr. Battle' stuff again. It's 'Chris.'"

"Okay, *Chris*, I still don't care what you do or where you do it."

She spoke without emotion, except maybe a trace of smugness, and hung up on him. Chris leaned back against the headboard and made a face. Well, wasn't *she* full of wit and charm? Har-di-har-har. She'd driven him out of his mind with that luscious body of hers and here he'd invited her to dinner to try to make amends for giving her a hard time—and what did he get? Smart-mouthed. That's what he got. Just plain smart-mouthed.

Didn't she know with whom she was dealing?

"Okay, *Chris*, I still don't care what you do or where you do it," he mimicked. But he couldn't get the tone right. Thought she was funny, did she? He exhaled and flopped back down on the bed. "You deserved it, Battle."

Yes, he had.

But he'd deserved a lot of other nasty things he'd had thrown at him over the years, and he'd managed to survive. Thrive, even.

He rolled over, grabbed the phone and dialed her number once more. This time her machine answered. "I know you're there," he said, but she still didn't pick up the receiver. He tried being conciliatory. "Hey, why don't we have dinner and talk this out? I'm sure we can work something out."

For his peacemaking efforts he received the beep of her answering machine. He gave up. He had another idea, which the mind that people all over the country called brilliant and incisive told him had to be one of his worst. Out and out nuts. But he didn't care. He dialed room service. Did they serve the condos? They did. Terrific. He ordered a magnificent dinner for two, complete with wine, an appetizer, dessert and after-dinner brandy and had it delivered to Page B. Harrington's condominium, compliments of Mr. Battle.

He'd shame her into inviting him up.

PAGE DEBATED SENDING the entire meal back with a message for Chris Battle to go soak his head. Or no message at all, just a stony silence. Either way, he'd have to get the point: she wasn't going to have anything more to do with him. But the food smelled delicious and looked wonderful, and all she had in her refrigerator was some leftover black bean soup. Well, why not?

Besides, she had an idea.

With a smile and a fat tip she accepted the expensive, elegant dinner. Half she wrapped carefully and put in the refrigerator. Battle's intentions lacked any subtlety; she knew the meal was meant as a "peace offering." He undoubtedly expected her to be so touched—in the heart or head, it didn't matter which—that she'd invite him to join her.

But Battle was wrong. Page saw the meal as another form of harassment, more palatable than the phone messages and parking himself at the pool while she did her laps, but still harassment.

Normally she didn't go for vengeance. It lacked maturity and was essentially a waste of energy. But...what could she say? It was almost spring. Something had to get her through the last days of winter—and Christopher O. Battle was asking for it.

Her half of the dinner she enjoyed tremendously, alone in her dining room with her daffodils, her view of the Garden, the lights of Beacon Hill beyond and Mozart playing quietly on her stereo. So civilized. So lonely. But she consoled herself by imagining Chris Battle pacing in his hotel room, waiting for her to call.

When she finished her dinner, she poured herself a glass of the brandy he'd sent up and, returning to the living room, dialed the front desk, which transferred her call to the combative journalist's room. Feeling full and languid, she sank into the soft cushions of her couch. She could hear his irritation just in the way he picked up the phone and snarled, "Battle," as if he were ready for one.

"Well, hello," she said cheerfully. She planned to lay it on thick. "I just wanted to say thank you so much for dinner. It was such a charming mea culpa. And sending enough for two was a stroke of real . . . well, chivalry, I suppose. Now I don't have to cook tomorrow night, either. Frankly, I hadn't thought you capable of such generosity. How very thoughtful."

He didn't say a word. *Ha*, Page thought, *choke, you smug bastard!* The meal had to have put him back well over two hundred dollars, but he could afford it. And, she reminded herself, he deserved to pay. She wasn't going to be the butt of anyone's joke.

She asked sweetly, "Mr. Battle, are you all right?"

"I only have one thing to say."

He did sound a bit enraged. Page beamed. "What's that?"

"This," he said darkly, "is war."

"What? *No*—"

"That's it. That's all I have to say."

"No, wait. We're even!"

"Even? *Even*? Lady, we're not even close to even."

And this time he hung up on her.

Well, Page thought, she'd got what she deserved, hadn't she? Chris Battle wasn't going to give up on her now! But as she sat back on her couch with her brandy, she wondered if that wasn't what, on some remote, unconscious level, she'd been after all along. She was goading him and she knew it. More to the point, she was enjoying herself. So many men she intimidated with her success as a businesswoman, her intensity, her togetherness. She didn't need a man to sweep her off her feet and rescue her from herself. She didn't need a man to do a nasty column on her that would appear in hundreds of newspapers all over the country, either, but at least Battle was willing to take her on her own terms—not that it would lead to anything romantic. He wasn't her type. Probably she wasn't his type. He would want someone he did intimidate.

"They always do," she muttered.

Never had she acted so impulsively, without thought for the consequences of her actions. Under ordinary circumstances, Battle seemed to have an unhealthy measure of determination. If anything, her behavior had *increased* that determination. Where was her common sense?

Floating on a spring breeze likely enough, she thought, trying to restore that feeling of victory with a sip of brandy.

CHRIS HAMMERED his left palm with his right fist as he paced back and forth in his room, looking for something not too expensive to kick. Page B. Harrington had already cost him enough, and declaring war on her didn't *touch* his frustration with her. Whenever he thought of his dinner sitting in her refrigerator, he felt a new wave of outrage inundate him. Never had he encountered a woman so thoroughly infuriating and so damn sneaky. She might even be sneakier than he was, which was saying something, indeed. And sweet. He grunted. She was about as sweet as a moray eel.

Even. Like hell they were even.

"I ought to go up there and break down her damn door."

But those weren't his tactics, and there was nothing to be gained in pretending they were. He preferred to use his wit and cunning. To do his article, he had to get inside her apartment and see her office, how she worked. He had to get inside her head. Tactics didn't interest him, except to the extent that there were those, such as brute force, that he wouldn't use. But he liked to get what he wanted. His readers trusted him to be thorough, if not objective, although he didn't pull any punches. They always knew where he was coming from, what his biases were. And, most important, that he'd do what had to be done to get the job done right.

He ordered a club sandwich from room service and avoided the thought of the two-hundred-dollar meal he'd paid for and Page B., the witch, had eaten. Slowly the tension in his muscles began to ease, and a certain spot inside him, a spot he didn't like to confront, forced him to wonder if professional pride wasn't only one part of his war with Page B. Harrington.

"Admit it," he said with a low growl, losing patience with himself, "you're having fun with this."

All right. He'd admit it. But it was still war.

When his sandwich came, he poured much of his lingering aggravation into a column he was writing on political corruption. But he found himself wondering what the *B* in Page B. Harrington stood for. Barracuda?

THE FOLLOWING MORNING, before she left for Cambridge and the nonprofit children's organization, Page checked with the front desk and was informed that Chris Battle had already checked out.

She did not breathe a sigh of relief.

3

THEY WERE BACK at the Newbury Street restaurant with the raw vegetable menu and the nice books of matches, but this time at Chris's expense. He'd called his friend William Norton that morning and talked him into lunch. A lumbering, curly-haired man, William had an intense, creative mind and an awesome visual memory, the primary reason he'd survived work habits even Chris considered chaotic. By shutting his eyes, William would visualize what he was looking for and remember where it was. Chris thought that was a neat trick. Who needed Get It Together Inc. and its turquoise-eyed proprietor?

"Your organizing woman made it possible so that you don't have to do your visualizing act, right?" Chris asked as idly as he could. Even after three days he still burned whenever he thought about Barracuda Harrington and *his* dinner. Conjuring her up in her black swimsuit and pink glasses was some consolation, but he didn't have the precision of William's visual memory. Once Chris touched something, however, it was his. Sometimes his fingers tingled when he imagined them brushing the soft swell of Page Harrington's breasts. He knew such thinking was dangerous. How could he explain *that* bias to his readers? But since when had he wanted to stop living dangerously?

"No, no," William said, digging into his salad of marinated mushrooms, blue cheese, red peppers and Lord knows what else. "Page helped me to get organized in a way that suits me and my personal idiosyncrasies. I told her I don't do lists, and she said, okay, fine, I could learn to organize myself using my visual skills. All I have to do is envision myself going through the next day or week, whatever, and use that as a basis for going about and getting things done."

"Prioritize?" Chris suggested wryly.

"Yeah. But Page hates that word."

So did Chris, but he refused to make too much of it. He tried some of his pasta primavera. A little heavy on the vegetables, but not bad. His natural perversity led him to crave fried onion rings whenever he was in a place like this.

"Everyone has priorities," William went on. "Sometimes it's just a question of sorting them out. Admit it, Chris. You have priorities, too, just like the rest of us."

"Sure. My priority is whatever I happen to be doing at the moment."

William shook his head in mock despair. "I'd love to see what happened if Page ever got hold of you."

"So would I, but I tried. She turned me down cold."

"Too big a job even for her?" William was grinning now.

"She's got it into her head I'm planning to make fun of professional organizers in my column."

"Are you?"

"Yeah."

"Then she's smart to stay away from you. I hope you're not planning to make me sorry I gave you her name."

"Come on, it's all in good fun. We're not talking money laundering here."

"Maybe. But Page takes what she does seriously."

"Maybe too seriously. You have to admit this is too good to pass up. Do you know there's actually a national organization of professional organizers? I love it: an organization for organizers."

William regarded his friend with open suspicion. "They've helped a lot of people—me, for one."

"Who says they haven't? Look, relax. I'm just trying to get a handle on what kind of person organizes other people for a living. Keeping my own life in order is enough of a chore without tackling someone else's. Is Page B. Harrington better than the rest of us? Or is she just compulsive and meddlesome? Or is this really just some kind of scam, a glorified, expensive way to get people to clean out their closets? I'm not going into this with my mind made up."

"Go on, Chris, you are, too."

He shrugged. "Well, okay, so I'm leaning toward thinking professional organizers are pretty silly. But that's not what I'm really trying to get at. I just want to lay out the facts and let my readers draw their own conclusions. Just do a straight up, simple column. I'll describe Page and what she does, quote her definition of it and her reasons for getting into this racket, describe her office and her apartment and . . . well, that's it. No commentary from me. I'll just let the descriptions and her quotes speak for themselves."

"Only because she turned you down as a client. Otherwise you'd nail her with your commentary."

"Probably."

William stabbed another mushroom, his suspicion unabated. "So why are you giving me this sob story instead of working on her?"

"What makes you think—"

"Chris, I've known you a long time. You don't call up for lunches at places like this on the spur of the moment without an ulterior motive. If we were drinking beer and eating burgers, maybe I'd believe you just needed an ear. So cut the act, okay, and tell me what you want."

Chris sighed. "Subtlety isn't my strong suit."

"No, it isn't."

"I can't get into her office. She won't return my phone calls and told the security people in her building that I'm bad news. They've thrown me out twice, and if I'm stupid enough to show up again without express permission from Ms Organizer herself, they're pressing harassment charges."

William waved a hand for a refill of his brewed decaffeinated coffee, something Chris refused to put to his lips. "Would it be dumb to ask why you don't just give up?"

"William, have I ever given up?"

"Not that I know of. It's probably the biggest reason you've gotten as far as you have—blind determination."

Chris gave up on the pasta and polished off the last of a glass of too expensive wine. "Don't forget my wit and charm."

"You know what they say, Battle—cream and bastards rise. And you, my friend, ain't cream. If you were, I'd believe you were buying me lunch out of the goodness of your heart. But you and I both know I owe you.

You've never called in the chips for taking me in two years ago when I got laid off. Three weeks of sleeping on your couch. It was pure hell, but better than laying out my sleeping bag in a subway station. So what's it to be?"

"Look, you don't owe me."

"Yeah, I do."

"No, dammit. If I'm ever down and out, I want to know I can count on my friends without having to be indebted to them for life. No, William, this is an out-and-out bribe. Lunch, which you've already consumed, and front-row Celtics-Lakers tickets, which are at this very moment in my wallet."

William winced. "Nasty, Chris. Really nasty."

"Just get me into her condo. That's where she has her office. I need a description in order to do my column the way I want to do it."

"You'll be nice?"

"William." Chris feigned being cruelly insulted. "I'm always nice."

"Yeah, right. I haven't been to a Celts game in ages. Front row?"

"Behind the Celtics bench."

"You drive a hard bargain, Battle. But I'll tell you this. I like that woman. She cares, and that's more than you can say for most people. You hurt her—"

"And I'll have to answer to you," Chris said, finishing for his friend.

"No." William grinned and wagged a finger at Chris. "No, pal, you'll have to answer to *her*. And in case you haven't noticed, that's one lady who can take care of herself. If she couldn't, I wouldn't succumb to your bribery."

Chris no longer felt quite so victorious. Had he for once taken on more than he could handle? Well, in for a penny, in for a pound. He'd just have to wait and see.

PAGE DIDN'T for a single second think she'd seen the last of Chris Battle. She was aware of his attempts to sneak into her condominium and assumed he needed to get into her office for some aspect of his column on professional organizers. But that was his problem. She wasn't going to cooperate. As far as she was concerned, the nasty journalist was on his own.

Which worried her. He seemed capable of anything. What next?

To help her sort out her options, she'd invited her friend Millie Friedenbach to afternoon tea in the Four Seasons lounge. They sat on the elegant upholstered chairs overlooking the Public Garden across Tremont Street. The warm spell had deteriorated into cold, sunny weather more typical of February, although Page didn't think there was anything "typical" about New England weather at any time of the year, except that it could "typically" be counted upon to change.

A pianist played softly, and tea was served on English bone china. It was all so civilized. Scones, jams, clotted cream, tiny sandwiches, pots of Earl Grey tea. Chris Battle would have wanted a hamburger, no doubt.

"I just don't know what he'll try next," Page lamented.

Millie nodded thoughtfully. She was a tall, big-boned woman with pale blond hair and giant blue eyes. She had been a member of the Boston University crew team as an undergraduate and still liked to go sculling alone on the Charles River—when she found the time. Divorced for two years, she had a six-year-old daughter and a demanding job as a buyer for an upscale downtown department store. That she was not material for a *Vogue* cover had never bothered her. Her earliest memory, she claimed, was of bouncing two neighborhood boys off the front porch for calling her fatso. That had given her more satisfaction than any compliments on her eyes or whatever. She believed in revenge. She was a strong woman, hardworking and attractive in all the ways that counted.

She was also honest to a fault. Leaning over to dab clotted cream onto a scone, she asked, "What do you want him to try?"

"Nothing!"

"That so?"

"Yes, of course. The man's an outrage."

"Good-looking outrage, though, isn't he?"

"In a crude sort of way, I suppose. But his looks are of no consequence to me."

"Don't pull that prim-and-proper act with me, Page. It's been a long time since your eyes have sparkled over a man."

"They're not sparkling."

"No?"

"No, they're..." She thought for a moment. "They're icing over."

"Get out of here. The guy sounds interesting."

"In all the wrong ways."

"Not your idea of Mr. Right?"

"Absolutely not. Perish the thought. Millie, I can't believe I've been sitting here for an entire hour explaining what Chris Battle has done to my life and it hasn't sunk in that I want nothing to do with him. Haven't I been making myself clear?"

Millie ate the scone and refilled her cup with tea, made from loose-leaf tea and not, mercifully, tea bags. Because she planned to lift weights later while her daughter, Beth, was at pottery class, she'd gobbled up everything in sight. Millie Friedenbach didn't believe in diets; she believed in exercise. "Yeah, yeah," she said, "I hear you. I'm just not sure I believe you. I think, Page, you'll be disappointed if this guy doesn't try something new."

"I won't, either. I've ignored him for three whole days."

"Wow."

"He's relentless."

"Well, there you go. You two do have something in common."

"We have *nothing* in common. He's not relentless in any way that's positive. He— Oh, never mind. Why did I invite you over for tea, anyway?"

Millie grinned. "Because you hate pity."

Page grinned back, laughing. "You're right—and God knows I've never gotten any from you! What do you think I should do?"

"Whatever you want to do."

"I need a plan."

"Some things you can't organize, you know. You might think you have a system for dealing with everything and everyone, but—"

"But not Chris Battle?"

"Not from the sound of it."

Millie had to run. If she was going to be in shape for spring rowing, she couldn't sit around with Page "yapping like a couple of junior high girls." She said she hoped being an ear helped, and she slipped off with a couple of extra sandwiches for Beth, who already took after her mother in size and appetite.

Trust Millie for an honest opinion, Page thought after her friend had left. She slowly drank a final cup of tea, watching pedestrians pass by on the wide sidewalk outside. She'd concluded her business with her Cambridge clients and had spent the early part of the afternoon doing paperwork. Trying to, at least. For reasons she wasn't sure she wanted to understand, she was totally preoccupied with Christopher O. Battle. Finally she'd called Millie to come over to tea, hear her tales of woe and have her say in no uncertain terms, "Forget the jerk."

But that wasn't what had happened. Usually Page was the one who listened and Millie the one who talked, but today had been different. Somehow, despite Page's schoolgirl protestations, Millie had sensed her friend's attraction to Battle. Her unexpected, inexplicable attraction. It was more an obsession, and a dangerous one at that. All she had to do was let down her guard for even a moment and he'd pounce. He'd make her and what she did the butt of one of his columns. All across the nation people would be snickering at professional organizers. She owed it to herself and her colleagues not to let that happen.

Yet something about his smile, his irreverent charm, stirred her physically and emotionally, and she wondered if what was going on wasn't simply the primitive, unpredictable longing for a solid male presence in her life. Not, of course, that Chris Battle was it. He was all wrong for her particular life. He just wouldn't fit. He didn't fit her life-style; he didn't fit her temperament; he didn't fit her preconceived notions of what kind of man *would* fit. He just stirred things up, that was all. And she wasn't sure what to do about it.

She supposed she did have a system for everything, including falling in love. It would be a civilized process. As yet, little that had gone on between her and Battle could be called civilized. He would be—and so would she—open, sincere, understanding. They would be adults. *Normal* adults. Chris Battle wasn't normal. He wasn't open; he was sneaky. He wasn't sincere; he was deceitful. He wasn't understanding; he was opinionated.

And Page B. Harrington, she reminded herself, was too smart to fall for a sneaky, deceitful, opinionated man.

Even if he was sexy as hell.

Even if she did wonder if she was being too hard on him.

Even if something about him—she couldn't pinpoint what—touched a corner of her soul that didn't respond to slate eyes and tanned shoulders, that said there was something about him that just might be right.

If she continued to ignore him, would he just give up? What if he did? *Then* what?

She finished her tea, paid the bill and went back up to her office. Unanswered questions, the inability to follow through on an idea and carry it to its logical conclusion, were danger signs, in her opinion signals of disorganization—of chaos. But she left her questions about Chris Battle unanswered, anyway.

And that, she thought, was the central problem with having him messing around in her life, stirring things up: he was turning it into chaos.

BY 6:30 Chris had begun to wonder if William had chickened out and let his natural considerateness prevail over his yearning for a little fun, but then his buzzer sounded, and in two minutes a sheepish-looking William Norton was standing in the entry.

"You can't let her know this was my doing," he said, shaking his head in self-reproach. "I can't believe I'm selling her out for Celtics tickets."

Chris resisted a grin of victory and tried instead to look the sympathetic friend. "Hey, you're human."

"Yeah. Well, at least now we're even."

"I told you, this is bribery. You don't and didn't owe me a damn thing."

"You're not making me feel any better, Chris."

Before William could change his mind, Chris fished the tickets out of his wallet and handed them over. Sighing guiltily, William retrieved an envelope from his pocket. Chris plucked it from his fingertips and promptly inspected the contents: inside, as promised, was the faked memo from Page B. Harrington, on her very "own" stationery. In the kind of perfunctory style she no doubt used—Chris had given William the exact wording—the memo gave permission for Christopher O. Battle to go up to her condominium to deliver a package of "critical importance."

"William, my friend, this is great. You'd have made one tough forger to nail down. Glad your mind doesn't run toward the less than honorable."

"It obviously does. Lord, Chris, I feel like such a traitor."

"She'll never know, and I'll behave, I promise."

"Right."

"Don't sound so dejected. Just name me one person who could resist Celtics tickets."

"I should be able to."

"Get going. You want to get there early enough to see the warm-ups. Have a hot dog for me, okay?"

"Chris—"

"Out, William. The deed is done."

He muscled William out the door and locked it behind him, wondering just how much his buddy was going to enjoy the game. *All to a good cause, my friend, all to a good cause.* Chris tore open a supply closet and dug around for an empty box. Couldn't find one. Not to let such a trivial annoyance dampen his good spirits, he dumped out a box of narrow-ruled canary pads and used it. He cut up a paper bag and wrapped the empty box very neatly and professionally. Appearances counted. Then with a black marker he printed Page B. Harrington's name and address on the front and stuck on a few red urgent stickers some joker had sent him for Christmas one year. He'd never had call to use them.

He paused and admired his handiwork. Perfect. But what if security demanded to know the contents of the box? He couldn't imagine they would, but given his record with them, he figured he'd best be prepared. What would a professional organizer need special-delivered? Paper clips, file folders, space organizers, calendars, rubber bands—none of that seemed urgent enough.

Then he had it. By God, did he ever!

Chuckling to himself, he tucked the bogus package under his arm and William's envelope in his jacket pocket and headed out.

PAGE FROWNED at the telephone. "What special delivery package is on its way up?"

"It's from...let me see." There was a pause as the desk clerk checked her information. "From Desperately Disorganized Inc. of Des Moines, Iowa. Your delivery man had personal authorization from you to bring the package up. I went ahead and sent him. Will there be a problem?"

There would definitely be a problem. Page had never heard of anything remotely called Desperately Disorganized Inc. of Des Moines, Iowa. If she'd authorized a delivery from such a company, she'd have remembered.

Her frown deepening, she wondered what Chris Battle was up to this time. "No, there won't be a problem. He's on his way up?"

"Yes, I—"

"A not too tall, not too handsome man?"

The desk clerk laughed. "Aren't they all?"

"But this one . . ."

"This one's different. Yeah, that's him. Security says he's the guy who's been bothering you the past couple of days. But according to the memo...I mean, it looked authentic."

"I'm sure it was." Battle was nothing if not thorough. "Please don't worry. I'll handle this."

Even as she hung up, her doorbell rang. After tea with Millie and exercise, Page had changed into a bright yellow jumpsuit and turquoise sneakers—a failed attempt to revive that vague, indescribable feeling of the first **taste** of spring. She had finished the last of the sinful almond torte Battle had chosen for dessert to the dinner he'd sent up the other night; she'd divided it so that she could spread it over three meals. One pot of daffodils was gone. The other was going.

She considered leaving her "delivery man" outside in the corridor. *He* could make excuses to security. But her reputation had suffered enough during the past week and . . . well, she admitted, she couldn't resist.

What wouldn't the man stoop to?

She tore open her front door.

He stood holding a package that appeared to be wrapped with a cut-up paper bag. But she took it in with little more than a glance as her gaze fell on the solid figure studying her. Chris Battle wore a rumpled corduroy jacket with a dark pullover underneath and battered twill pants that looked as if they'd seen safari duty. His hair was a tousled mess. A treacherous twist of her imagination flashed an image of him rising from bed in the morning with his hair in just that kind of mess. But no matter what her imagination threw at her, it couldn't rival Chris Battle in person. And given the vividness of her imagination the past few days, that was saying something.

But she was nothing if not self-disciplined. "You have a delivery for me?" she asked briskly.

"Well—"

"From Desperately Disorganized Inc.?"

"Look, I know what you think and I don't blame you—"

"Tax returns, correct? I promised I'd have a look. They said they'd rush them right out. Aren't they an unusual outfit? They've made a specialty of antiplanning humor. They write jokes for a number of late-night television shows—even their Des Moines address is part of their act, a gimmick of sorts. I find their humor in poor taste, of course, but who am I to judge? They like to hire me on occasion and then poke fun at how good I am at my work. Ingrates, don't you think?"

A deep frown of pure incredulity—shock, even— creased Battle's forehead. "I don't believe you."

"Yes, well, that's of no consequence to me, I'm sure. You don't make enough money writing your nasty columns that you have to moonlight as a delivery boy? A pity. Here, I'll take that."

She snatched the package from his hand, and before he could recover from his complete bafflement, she shut the door. Not exactly in his face. But close enough.

The doorbell rang once, twice, thrice.

She chuckled to herself. "Stand out there and rot, Mr. Battle."

She tossed the box onto her kitchen counter, proud of herself for having come up with a credible reason for a corporation called Desperately Disorganized Inc. to exist. But perhaps she'd only encouraged Battle.

The doorbell rang a fourth time.

She grabbed her pocket knife—a recommendation for all her clients, women included—and sliced open the package. Narrow-ruled pads, the box said. Inside was nothing at all.

The doorbell rang a fifth time. Then Battle pounded twice and yelled, "You're not going to get away with this!"

She couldn't resist. She walked to the door and peered through the peephole. Even as distorted as he appeared, she could tell she had one highly aggravated man on her threshold. Good, she thought.

"Mr. Battle," she said, her voice normal and calm, "I already did."

BACK OUT ON Tremont Street, Chris considered battering rams, parachute drops, napalm and simple breaking and entering to get into Page B. Harrington's condominium. When he did, he'd lay waste to the place. Tear everything out of her closets, dump out her drawers, empty her files, rip April and May out of her calendar, stick the *W*'s in with the *R*'s and the *A*'s in with the *F*'s in her Rolodex, throw out all her labels and all her things that held other things. She'd have to start living like a normal person.

For five minutes, maybe. She'd probably need at least that long to put everything right back where he'd found it. Organized people had *systems*. A place for everything, everything in its place. How many times growing up had he heard that neat dictum?

Forcing himself to calm down, Chris proceeded toward Copley Square, aimless. Page B. was good. He had to admit it. He'd expected her just to give up and let him in, get the messy business over with, but instead she'd faked him out in her bright yellow jumpsuit. What was that all about, anyway? And the turquoise shoes? To be sure, she had a logical reason for each.

And to be equally sure, he had zip. He'd been humiliated; he'd been threatened once more by security—the *last* time, they'd said—and he'd lost his Celtics

tickets. All he had for his troubles was an appetite.
Dammit, sparring with Ms Organizer made him hungry.

He grinned, a sudden, insane grin. "What the hell—
you're spontaneous, right?"

He found a pay phone, dialed Page B.'s number... and almost hung up when she answered. Her
voice did strange things to him, like make him remember her sleek body and expressive eyes instead of her
tripe about tax returns and antiplanning humor. What
the hell was that? Late-night shows. He'd give her antiplanning humor.

But he didn't hang up. "Hi, it's me."

"Who's me?"

"You know, dammit. Your cutesy-poo act is wearing
real thin. Want to cut it and meet me over at Durgin
Park for supper? Nothing fancy. I feel like digging my
teeth into something that won't bite back."

She laughed, a delicious sound that made his mouth
water, and he realized there was something else he
wouldn't mind digging his teeth into. But he didn't think
Page B. would be lured from her condo if he told her.
Of course, he didn't think Page B. would be lured from
her condo no matter what he told her.

He bit his tongue and kept quiet.

"You're serious?" she asked.

"Sure."

"I just ate the last of your almond torte."

"Don't remind me. I'm still smarting over that fiasco."

"What fiasco?"

"Page, you know damn well—"

"Your peace offering, you mean? But it was delightful!"

"*Page!*"

"My, aren't we familiar for a delivery boy?"

"Forget dinner."

"No, no. Give me thirty minutes."

"For what? You don't need to change. You looked fine to me. It's almost spring, right? Nobody'll notice a bright yellow jumpsuit and—"

"I'll meet you there," she interrupted once more. "If I don't show, it means I've talked myself out of this display of total insanity. You're dangerous, Christopher Battle."

"Me! Who just got tossed from one of Boston's swankiest hotels courtesy of one turquoise-eyed barracuda? Lady, you're the one who's dangerous."

She had started laughing again. Definitely a mouthwatering laugh. Spine-tingling, even. A pity she was so compulsively organized.

"Don't talk yourself out of coming, okay?"

He surprised himself by how serious he sounded. What was going on here? Alarms went off inside the part of his brain still functioning in its cynical columnist mode, warning him not to get too close. He ignored them and debated his next move as he headed toward Copley Place at a slow, thoughtful pace. But then he reminded himself that organized people were the ones who weighed pros and cons before doing anything. He wasn't organized; he was spontaneous.

So he'd just wing dinner with Ms Barracuda.

4

As she rode the main escalator up to the second floor of shops at Copley Place, Page considered forgetting dinner altogether and heading over to Neiman-Marcus to check out what was on sale. Boston's first indoor mall, sandwiched between venerable Copley Square and the revived South End, Copley Place had opened in 1984 to considerable hoopla with high-priced and specialty shops. Even though the mall was within easy walking distance of her condominium, Page wasn't one to fritter away her time shopping. But tonight, she was tempted.

She'd eaten at the original Durgin Park at Faneuil Hall Marketplace a few times and had enjoyed the unique atmosphere of the restaurant, famous for its "surly" waiters and waitresses, its family-style service and its refusal to accept checks, credit cards or reservations. The Copley Place version wasn't as rough around the edges, but she'd never checked it out herself. Ordinarily she preferred small, quiet restaurants. But right now noise and crowds—witnesses—seemed like a good idea to her. She wasn't sure how Chris Battle would exact his revenge for her not having let him get away with his delivery-boy act. But he'd no doubt try something. It seemed he always did.

He was sitting at a table along the rail in the outside section overlooking the second-floor marble plaza, which provided the place with the ambience of an indoor café. He didn't wave or smile, but Page knew he'd spotted her as she walked past him to the entrance. She could *feel* the effect of his gaze as a wave of buttery-warm sensations hit her lower back. Now that he knew she'd come this far, if she didn't go in, he'd fly out of there like the proverbial bat out of hell and haul her in himself. It might actually be interesting to have him try. He could have Copley Place security on his case just like the hotel security. Pretty soon there'd be nowhere left in Boston he could go. Page had to smile thinking of it. But she supposed she'd had her fair share of revenge for one night.

She just wasn't sure she was being smart in giving him the opportunity to get in *his* fair share of revenge. But after thinking over the delivery episode, she wondered if perhaps she'd misinterpreted his actions. What if he had, in fact, been trying in his own peculiarly warped way to make amends? She'd cut him off a number of times. Had he been trying to explain? Apologize? She hadn't given him a chance, but with her need to control the situation—her fear of not giving him an inch—how could she have let him into her apartment and left herself open to insult and ridicule? She had to remember that as much as she might be drawn to his dark eyes and deep voice and sexy grin, *he* was motivated by his own professional interests. He was Wile E. Coyote trying to chase down the Roadrunner. He was determined, he'd stop at nothing and he had to have his own way.

And she was nuts for having shown up.

Still, she thought it politic to get her butt inside.

Only vaguely, deep in the dark recesses of her mind, did it occur to her she might have some amends to make herself. But she didn't drag the thought out into the open and examine it. She left it back there, lurking.

Battle's eyes, mysterious, almost murky in the shadows of the restaurant, held hers as she manufactured a smile and made her way to the table. He seemed neither angry nor amused nor even pleased or displeased by what he saw, only strangely objective—as if he were keeping his feelings, his subjectivity, at bay. She felt him studying her, taking in what she wore, her looks, her expression, how she walked, everything he could and storing it all in that cynical mind. Probably thinking about how he'd describe her in his column.

She wasn't sure she liked feeling this way, like an amoeba on a slide under a microscope, like one of those poor slobs captured on camera by a tough, unrelenting reporter—not one of the pretty boys or pretty girls, but one of those hound dogs, male or female, who knew how to ferret out information. The Chris Battles of the world. They weren't meant to be pretty. Page tried to imagine him with all the wrong angles in his face smoothed over, all the wrinkles in his clothes pressed out, all the cynicism in his eyes gone. It wouldn't work. He'd be someone else. A different—a worse—kind of wrong.

But as she moved closer, Page saw that he wasn't viewing her with any objectivity whatsoever but was keeping a tight rein on his reaction to her. She could see the tensed muscles in his neck, the smoldering look in his eyes, the way he held one hand on his beer glass, rigid and carefully under control. She hadn't thought control was Chris Battle's strong suit. Perhaps it wasn't and he was using everything at his command to retain that control. But control over what? She didn't know what he was thinking, couldn't imagine or just didn't want to complicate her life by trotting out the possibilities. But whatever it was, it damn well wasn't how his beer tasted.

Keeping a tight rein on her own reactions, she slid into the chair opposite him.

He picked up his glass and took a sip of beer, licking his lips slowly and intentionally, as if he were licking her, and set the glass back down. "So you didn't have an attack of common sense."

"Actually I did. Not an attack, really—"

"Too disorderly." He smiled, warmth coming into his eyes as he teased her. "If you're attacked, it's by a lack of common sense."

She drank some ice water, feeling suddenly nervous and uncomfortable and, worse, not knowing why. "You're a know-it-all, aren't you?" she shot back, over-reacting to what had been nothing more than a gentle tease. Couldn't she laugh at herself? Sure. But being laughed at was another matter altogether. Or perhaps she was just more at ease when they were arguing. "You're no better than a playground bully always spoiling for a fight. Be that as it may, I reasoned that by joining you for dinner, I could perhaps convince you to quit this ridiculous assault on my privacy—"

She stopped and stared at him. He had leaned back in his chair and folded his arms across his chest, and was grinning broadly at her, his slate eyes gleaming. Her gaze dropped to the dark hairs on his wrists, then lifted back to his face. There were more sensations. Many more.

"What's the matter with you?" she demanded.

The grin didn't waver. "Do you always talk like a pompous ass?"

"Only when I'm dealing with one!"

"Quick," he said. "Very quick. My assorted 'ex-wives' would love you. They weren't as good at comebacks."

Inhaling deeply, Page forced herself not to stoop to his level. It would only be counterproductive. She *had* sounded a bit pompous, but only as a device to maintain some objectivity for herself. Reason and intuition both told her to treat Chris Battle as a textbook problem, not a living, breathing, *irritating* man.

"All right, look," she said, "we're both adults, and there's no need to reduce ourselves to a couple of squabbling adolescents. I understand you want to do a piece on professional organizers and that I'm your target and can't stop you from pursuing what you think is a legitimate idea. I can't control what I can't control."

"How astute. You make that up yourself?"

Her look darkened as she resisted the temptation to pour Mr. Christopher O. Battle's beer on his arrogant head. "Learning to recognize what you can't control is an important part of becoming more organized, one that's quite liberating, in fact. But I don't expect you to understand. I don't care that you don't. May I continue?"

He didn't look properly chastened but merely shrugged and motioned for her to proceed, the gleam still in his eyes. "Please. By all means continue."

"I wasn't asking for permission," she said hotly.

"I know. You were being sarcastic. I'm not stupid, Page B. I might not be organized, but don't ever think I'm stupid."

"What about reckless, inconsiderate, conceited, irritating, stubborn, close-minded—"

"Sure."

"But not stupid."

"Right."

She sighed. What had she gotten herself into?

"Go on," he said, and this time she saw he was biting back a smile and realized he had been at least half kidding. Was there no figuring the man? Didn't he even regard himself without a measured dose of cynicism?

"I thought we could make a deal."

He shook his head. "Journalists don't make deals."

"But you're not really a journalist. You're a columnist. That's different."

"Okay, then, *I* don't make deals."

"Mr. Battle—"

"Will you stop with the 'mister' already? It's 'Chris.' Would you call the playground bully 'mister'?"

"Chris," she said, hanging on to the last threads of her patience, "I'm calling what I'm offering a deal only because it sounds nicer. But it's not really a deal."

"Why doesn't that surprise me? It's your way or no way."

The man was an outrage. "It's an ultimatum."

"Oh-ho. Should I write this down?"

"I think you'll remember, and besides, I don't want to wait for you to find something to write with...or on."

"That's a low blow. Restaurants always have matchbooks, and I've got a pencil stashed in a pocket somewhere."

"Yes, but which one? Never mind. You're driving me crazy, you know that? One more interruption and I swear I'll—"

The waiter interrupted. With a sigh Page ordered roast turkey. Battle embarrassed her by ordering just a bowl of soup. But what could she do? She was hungry.

"My offer-deal-ultimatum is this," she continued, their order in, the waiter gone, nothing to interrupt her. "You can ask me two questions—any two questions you want. I'll answer them honestly and to the best of my ability. Then you go write your damn article and leave me alone."

"Now?"

"Now."

"I don't have my tape recorder with me."

"I'll give you time to find your pencil and tear open some matchbooks."

"But even if I did have my tape recorder," he went on, ignoring her gibe, "it wouldn't matter. I don't like offers, deals or ultimatums."

"Then you don't get anything out of me. I'm not going to help you get organized. I'm not going to talk to you about how I help other people get organized. I'm not going to tolerate your attempts to sneak into my home so you can write some nasty little piece on how I organize myself. In short, *Chris*, I'm not going to allow you to belittle me."

He tilted his head back, eyeing her through half-closed eyes, and again she found herself responding to his unbridled masculinity. She imagined the touch of his lips on hers and had to drink more ice water, just to cool off. She didn't need to fan the flames between them. She burned enough as it was.

"Why do you insist on thinking I'm going to belittle you?" he asked, his expression unchanged.

"Because you've already tried—and I read your column."

His eyes opened and he grinned. "Is that right?"

"Not with any joy, I assure you. It's hardly the first thing I turn to."

"You have a routine for reading the paper?"

"Well—"

He waved off her retort and leaned over, one hand very close to hers, tapping his fingertips on the table one at a time. "Page, I'm sorry," he said, his voice surprisingly soft. "I'm egging you on and I know it. It's just that professional organizers are so easy to poke fun at. That's the mind-set I have or had going into this thing. Get It Together Inc.—how could I resist? But that doesn't mean you can't change my mind. You obviously take yourself seriously. Show me what you do, show me how you do it and show me *why* you do it. Make *me* take you seriously."

She avoided his eyes...and his fingers. "Why should I?"

"Consider it a challenge."

His voice had lowered, deepened, and with his index finger he flicked drops of condensation off the outside of her water glass. It was a deliberate move. It didn't take a great leap of imagination for her to feel that same finger on her skin. Her nipples hardened at the thought, and she quickly folded her arms under her breasts, feeling their ache. The challenge he was presenting, she suspected, went beyond a simple column.

"I face challenges every day," she said, proud of the level sound of her voice. "Far more enticing challenges, I might add. I prefer to put my energy into helping people who need and want my help. All you want to do is make a buck off me."

He didn't appear taken aback as one eyebrow quirked and he leaned back in his chair. "Low, Page."

"Accurate."

"You want to know what I think?"

"No."

"*I* think you're afraid of me."

"Pshaw."

Battle smiled, the corners of his eyes crinkling, and she saw a crookedness about his mouth that she hadn't noticed before. It was both endearing and unexpectedly, undeniably sensual. The challenge was there, all right. *Take me on*, it said.

"Forget it, Chris." But she was really saying, *forget it, Page, you're not that crazy.* "I'm not afraid to take you on. I believe I've already proved that, don't you?"

"I didn't say you were afraid to take me on. I don't even think you're afraid of what I might write about you. What I said—and what I believe—is that you're afraid of *me*. You know I'm attracted to you on a physical level."

"Oh, right. You make fun of me and drive me nuts."

"That's just me doing my job. And being attracted to you on a physical level has nothing to do with making fun of you or driving you nuts. It has to do with—"

"Don't."

"See? Cold, hard fear, Page B. It's making your skin clammy, isn't it? You know damn well I'm sitting here fighting the urge to kiss you."

"Poor thing."

"Sarcasm won't get it. What would you do?"

"If you kissed me? I don't know. I can't imagine I'd let you get that far—that close, I should say. If you did, I guess I'd just smack you one."

"An organized response. I love your nonviolent approach. But I don't believe you. I think you'd kiss me back, and I think that's precisely what scares you—that you think you'd kiss me back, too."

She raised her chin and stared him down. "You're implying that this attraction business isn't just one-way."

"Uh-huh."

"Amazing. Just amazing. I'd have thought a columnist known for his incisiveness would demonstrate more of it, but we all make mistakes. I'm neither afraid of you nor attracted to you, and I'm sure as hell not afraid of myself or anything to do with our 'relationship,' such as it is."

Chris Battle regarded her with open skepticism, not believing her any more than she believed herself. They both knew she was lying. She was attracted to him, all right. His raw sensuality, the twist of his mouth, the gleam of his slate eyes, the sandy roughness of his voice, the quickness of his wit—they all combined to make him one difficult-to-resist male. His talk of kissing her had made her tingle with anticipation until she ached all over. But she didn't trust him. Wouldn't. Maybe he was attracted to her, but in none of the ways that mattered. Wanting to kiss her was one thing. The sexual tension that had been crackling and sparking between them since she'd heard his voice on her message machine could easily burst into a hot, open flame that consumed them both. It would be satisfying to burn up in his arms, to feel him burn up in hers. But then what? They were incompatible on every other level, and she was too organized and self-disciplined to permit herself to give in to a desire that was purely physical. She didn't need to complicate her life that way. Perhaps another woman would be willing to face the consequences, but that was another woman. She was Page B. Harrington and had to live with her limitations.

She didn't expect Chris would understand, and even if he did, why bother to explain? It was simpler to tell herself—and him—that he was just trying out another strategy to get into her condominium so he could write his column. Tell the woman he wants to kiss her and watch her melt.

It wouldn't work.

Even if it wasn't what he was doing.

"If that's the way you want it," he said, the grin vanishing as warmth, even sympathy, came into his expression. "I won't push."

"Thank you. Think about my offer. It'll stand until this time tomorrow."

"Okay, but my answer won't change."

Her dinner and his bowl of chowder arrived, but before they'd even got started, the waiter returned with a wrapped meal, which he set at Chris's elbow. Chris thanked him and just had a taste of his soup.

"Well," he said, as he got up, grabbed the wrapped dinner and tucked it under his arm, "this has been an interesting conversation, but I have to run. Enjoy your dinner—and thanks."

"For what? Wait just a minute! What's going on here?"

"I'm thanking you for dinner." He was obviously fighting a laugh. "And what's going on here, Ms Barracuda, is tit for tat—or almost. Durgin Park isn't as expensive as the Four Seasons."

"You mean you've—"

"I mean I've stuck you with the bill."

Page could feel her eyes narrowing. "You are a snake in the grass, Battle, and I'm glad I— Never mind. Just go."

He grinned at her, looking very pleased with himself, indeed. "You're glad you didn't tell me you think I'm sexy as hell, aren't you? Yeah, I'll bet you're damn glad."

"Battle—"

"I'll see you later."

"You're damn right you will!"

Raging, she watched him saunter off thinking he'd won. She'd have to show him—somehow. But when she turned back to her turkey dinner and saw his empty soup bowl and empty chair, she suddenly felt an emptiness inside herself. And she wondered if perhaps they both wanted their private little war to keep dragging on, just as an excuse to stay in each other's lives a bit longer. Because when the war ended, she thought, he'd return to his messy attic on one side of the Public Garden, she'd return to her tidy condominium on the other side, and whatever had been between them, or even *might* have been between them, would be just a memory.

All that would remain would be the emptiness.

TWO QUESTIONS SHE'D ANSWER from him. Chris grunted in disgust as he put his feet on his library table the afternoon following his aborted dinner with Ms

Organizer. His twenty-four hours were almost up, and he'd narrowed his list down to *twenty* questions. How could he limit himself to just two? Not that it mattered. He wasn't going to knuckle under to Page B.'s outrageous ultimatum. He was a journalist and had a responsibility to his editors, his readers, himself. He operated under a strict code of ethics that might not be immediately apparent to the targets of his wit but was to him. That code didn't include making deals with beautiful professional organizers. He didn't intend to climb on his moral high horse and give Page B. a host of reasons for turning her down. If for no other reason, he didn't want her to develop a good opinion of him. At least, not right now. Not while he was still working on her.

He looked out across the Public Garden. It was drizzly and blustery, but the red buds of the trees were beginning to open—just in time to be smacked by another snowstorm. Chris had opened his window a crack in hopes that the cold air would clear his head. A gust of wind had scattered a pile of receipts onto the floor. He'd get to them sometime. Right now he was thinking about Page's ultimatum and possible ways of getting around it. Using it to advantage.

In short, hoodwinking her.

No, he thought, *not just hoodwinking her...*

He wanted to see her again. If he really had to, he supposed he could go with what he had and write his column. Forget about seeing her office. Forget about talking to her. Just take broad swipes at her and her profession. Shouldn't be too hard, right? How in-depth did he have to be with professional organizers?

"Okay," he muttered aloud, "exactly what do you have?"

Turquoise eyes with dark lashes.
Wears contact lenses and swims laps and has a message machine.
And at times a sultry voice.
Her smile can melt ice and the spines of intrepid journalists.
Has a knack for getting people to clean up their acts.
And very nice legs.

He shook his head in despair as the heat of pent-up desire forced him to shift his position. "I'd like to see you print that. My man, you still don't know what makes the woman tick."

That could be question one: "Page B. Harrington, what makes you tick?"

No, too vague. Too unjournalistic. Something a potential lover might ask. As a nasty, witty syndicated columnist he had to find the answer without ever really posing the question. But which was he?

He gave a self-deprecating chuckle. "My man, are you seriously considering making love to a woman who probably color-codes her office?"

He was.

A blast of cool spring air brought him to his senses, and he snatched up the phone and tapped out her number. For once she answered instead of her machine.

"Page B." he said, kicking his feet back down onto the floor. Flat on the floor where, he reminded himself, they belonged. *You're a hard-bitten columnist, and professional organizers are this week's target.* "I've been rethinking your offer."

"Oh?"

So smug. But he admired her self-confidence. Took him on with style, she did. "Yeah," he said, hoping he sounded equally smug. *A match for you, sweets.* "I've got the two questions you can answer honestly and to the best of your ability, as you promised. Okay?"

"Okay. . . I think."

"You sound suspicious."

"I can't imagine why."

He could hear her sarcasm; he'd have to be an idiot not to. "Really?"

"Don't make me regret this."

But that was the whole idea. Ah, cursed plans—such as they were. He was winging it yet again. He had no idea what he wanted to ask her, just that he didn't want the twenty-four hours to slip away, *her* to slip away. Column or no column, he wasn't finished with Page B. Harrington.

"First question," he said, using his tough-journalist voice and feeling a surge of anticipation. By God, he loved taking on this woman. "You're an organized person in your own right, correct?"

"It took some work, but yes. Your second question?"

"No, wait, dammit. That was just a preliminary to my first question—"

"Was it or wasn't it a question, Mr. Journalist?"

"Look here—"

"Your second question."

"All right, be like that. You didn't answer to the best of your ability, as you promised you would. 'It took some work.' What does that mean?"

"It means I wasn't always organized."

"You used to live in chaos?"

Hell. He felt like the poor slob who'd just used up the genie's three wishes without having realized it.

"That's your *third* question, but I'll be reasonable. Yes, I did live in a sort of chaos. When I was a child, my family always seemed to be overwhelmed by life, one step away from disaster, never able to cope with the demands placed on us with the limitations we faced in terms of time, money, space and character. I find deep satisfaction in helping people make the best of what they have rather than always to be waiting for the pot of gold at the end of the rainbow. If I just get this or do that or have more time or more space or whatever, *then* I can get organized, *then* I can live a less stressful life, *then* I can be happy. It's strange how much happier people can be when they just can find a spatula when they need one. There, satisfied?"

"No. Those weren't the questions I wanted to ask." *Dammit*, he thought, *I should have known not to come at her without a plan.*

"Too bad. I'll look forward to reading about professional organizers in your column. I'm sure we'll survive being butchered by Chris Battle. Others certainly have."

A gust of wind cooled him off, but only a little. Page B. had a knack for keeping his blood boiling. "You want to leave it like this?"

"Sure. I've kept my end of the deal."

He didn't hear even a note of tentativeness in her voice. Had he mistaken a desire to get rid of him for a desire—at least the beginnings of one—to go to bed with him? Was he that big of an egotist?

"Aren't you even a tiny bit curious as to what my real two questions were?"

"Curiosity is a waste of time," she said in that pomp-ous-ass voice he now could recognize as fake—a cover for what she was really feeling and didn't want to ad-mit to. Hearing it reassured him she wasn't sure after all that she wanted to be finished with him. "Anything else?"

"Why are you doing this to me?"

"That's question four, and I'm just not that gener-ous. Too bad, isn't it? Goodbye, Mr. Battle. Perhaps I'll bump into you in the Garden someday. Um, good luck with your piece. I'm sure it will be as annoying as you can make it."

She hung up, having the last word yet again.

Chris would have thrown something out his win-dow toward hers if it might have had any chance of hitting, but with his present luck, it'd just bonk off some tourist's head and he'd get arrested. He was doomed. He'd taken on a woman in every way a match for him. She'd answered his "two questions." She'd even given him some material he could use in his column. But she'd also further intrigued him. It was no longer profes-sional curiosity and instinct that motivated him. Other stuff had come into it days ago—the turquoise eyes, the long legs—but that was just physical attraction, al-though there seemed no "just" about it. But he hadn't expected to find Page B. witty and gutsy in addition to sexy, and now she was proving to be, in her own way, sympathetic and even interesting. He hadn't expected a professional organizer to be interesting. A woman who helped people organize their lives and put their spatulas where they could find them when they wanted to flip a pancake. *I find deep satisfaction in helping people make the best of what they have . . .* What did she mean, specifically? How did she do that, specifically?

"Who are you, Page B.?"

He had to know. And even if journalistic curiosity and instinct had little to do with his motives, he was determined he would find out.

THAT NIGHT a nor'easter blew in first with rain, then sleet, then snow. Page was awakened by the howling of the wind and made herself a cup of cocoa, which she drank in her living room while looking out across the Public Garden toward Beacon Hill. She could see a light in Chris's attic window. Had he simply forgotten to turn it off? Invited a woman friend over? Or, like her, couldn't sleep? He was even more unpredictable than New England weather—and he could be just as treacherous.

But more than likely he was burning the midnight oil because he had to meet a deadline and hadn't paced himself properly. He was a man who responded to pressure. He needed a tough deadline to rub up against to get his adrenaline flowing. Life with such an individual would have to be impossible.

No wonder the ex-wives.

Possibly he was pulling an all-nighter to finish his piece on professional organizers. Well, she thought, let him. She wasn't going to further involve herself with a man with his peculiarities. She couldn't. Physical attraction just wasn't enough, and she was determined to resist it. She had so far, hadn't she?

She knew she was driving herself crazy. For the first time in months she was actually distracted from her work. It was frustrating. Dangerous. But the fact remained that although curiosity was a waste of time and Chris Battle a threat to her stability, she was damned if she didn't want to know what his two questions were. She was convinced he hadn't reneged on his decision not to take her up on her offer and that somehow his two questions were designed to stick it to her—only she'd been onto his scheme yet again. "Deals" just weren't his style. She hadn't expected him to have any sense of what she would call honor—anything for a story, a fact, a quote, seemed more his modus operandi. Had she misjudged him?

No. He *had* called with two questions, hadn't he? Just because she didn't for a second believe they were two legitimate questions didn't make what he'd done more honorable. He was using her ultimatum to get *around* her ultimatum . . . which did, she suppose, have a certain odd logic.

Only it hadn't worked. Instead of his sticking it to her, she'd stuck it to him.

It was a small and surprisingly hollow victory. She'd left him with no recourse and might, in fact, never see him again and—

The column! *That* could be his recourse.

Her gaze drifted toward the window and the light in the attic on Beacon Street, and she shuddered, wondering if perhaps she was being slightly premature in feeling sorry for Christopher O. Battle.

5

"I'VE BEEN FOUND OUT."

William sounded worried and a little angry over the telephone. Chris was reheating a mess of Chinese food for lunch after a disastrous morning of work. He couldn't get a handle on his latest column. Every lead he wrote sounded so namby-pamby. Sickening. But he was almost getting used to rotten mornings. In the two weeks since Page B. Harrington had had the "last" word with her two-question ultimatum, he'd stayed away from her. No more calls, no more sneaking into her building, no more bright ideas on how to get past her unequivocal desire to have nothing whatsoever to do with him. The woman didn't like him. Ordinarily that would have been a damn good reason to keep at her. More likely than not, her distaste would lead to better material for his column. But it wasn't that simple: she didn't like him, but she *did* want to go to bed with him. And he with her. And that, curse his soul, complicated everything. It meant no column, and it meant no being a bastard. He wasn't going to foist himself upon a woman who wanted him but didn't like him.

Yet apparently he wasn't going to forget about her, either. It was a dilemma, and he didn't know what the hell to do. Obviously she knew: she was staying out of his life. He didn't like to admit how disappointed he was.

"Found out about what?" he asked, smelling the spicy chicken with orange sauce. Since meeting Page he'd taken to hot, spicy foods. Gave him a similar sort of rush that being with her did, but it wasn't the same. Spicy food didn't make him burn in quite the same places as she did. "Have you been embezzling funds or stealing pencils? What?"

"Page."

Chris didn't say a word, just stood very straight as the microwave dinged. Page . . .

"Page Harrington. You remember."

His heart pounded. Yes, he remembered. But he said lightly, "Barracuda Harrington?"

"Chris, for God's sake, this is serious. She called me about five minutes ago and said she'd put two and two together and come up with the snake-in-the-grass client who'd finked on her to you. Said I was a Judas. She's . . . she's on her way over. I think she might be bringing hot tar and feathers."

Why did Chris want to laugh? Why did he want to jump up and clap his hands? Was he *nuts*?

No, just reenergized. Page B. Harrington hadn't dismissed the goings-on of a couple of weeks back as an "unfortunate incident"—her kind of phrasing—but had pursued the person who'd betrayed her. Not something a self-disciplined, organized, never-do-anything-without-a-purpose woman would do. What did she hope to accomplish by tracking down William? Revenge? Not her style. A waste of time. No way. There was no logical reason for her to drag William out on the carpet. It was an illogical act.

An act of a woman who hadn't been able to get one nasty ol' journalist off her mind. Considering said mind, that was something, indeed.

And now she'd as much as invited herself back into his life.

"You want me to come over?" he asked.

"*No!* Stay the hell out, will you? I just called to let you know the Celtics tickets weren't worth it. I couldn't enjoy the game because I felt like such a sneak, and I didn't have anybody interesting to go with and keep my mind off what I'd done—and the Celts lost."

"William, William, you told me about Page Harrington all in good faith, remember? You didn't sell her out for tickets. That wasn't until *after* she and I had met."

"Thanks a lot," William said, sarcastic and dispirited. "Next time I need a shoulder to cry on, I'll remember who not to call."

"I'll be there in fifteen minutes."

"Don't—"

"Trust me, William. Page'd be disappointed if I didn't show."

"Do *not* come by here. I mean it—"

"Bruins tickets. Tonight's game against the Canadiens. Seats are behind the penalty box."

"Chris, how could you?"

"Come on, William."

"I haven't seen a hockey game in . . ."

"I'll bring the tickets with me," Chris said, and hung up.

With a little hoot of victory he stabbed a chunk of chicken with a fork. It tasted great. Hot, spicy, tangy. But he left the plate in the microwave and headed out.

Page B. was a match for Chinese orange chicken any day.

WILLIAM NORTON'S OFFICE was on upper Newbury Street near the venerable Ritz and easy walking distance from Page's condominium, where she'd returned after meeting with clients on the waterfront that morning. She'd taken the subway home. It was a beautiful spring day—the six inches of snow from the last nor'easter had long since melted—and all over town Boston's famous magnolias were budding. Before long they'd be in full bloom. They had a dangerous effect on her. Brought on the strange restlessness and full, emotional feelings of spring fever. Made her think of things better not thought of, like Chris Battle.

She'd had to shove aside yet another vivid image of him in his skimpy bathing trunks as she'd climbed onto a Green Line car. All she'd wanted to do was get back to her office and dive into a planned afternoon of paperwork.

But during the short ride to Boylston Street Station, she'd again tackled the issue of who had ratted on her. Who had given Chris Battle her name in the first place? Who had provided him with a perfect replica of her memo stationery? Who would be that sneaky, that duplicitous, that much under Battle's influence? Who would *owe* Battle more than he or she owed Get It Together Inc.?

The traitor had to be a former client, she'd reasoned. But she prided herself on the loyalty of her clients. Many were her friends. How—

The name William Norton had jumped out at her on the subway, and she couldn't say why it had then and not before.

Of course.

He was a recent client, a creative advertising genius who knew everybody. She'd helped organize the drawer where for years he'd been tossing scraps of paper with phone numbers jotted on them, business cards, torn tops of stationery, old address books, envelopes, *memos*. That he knew Chris Battle would be no surprise to her. That he'd kept an old memo of hers, despite his reformed habits, would also be no surprise to her.

That he'd *ratted* on her, the fink, was a surprise, but she did know how persuasive Battle could be.

After she'd done it, she didn't understand why she'd called William and screamed at him and said she was on her way over. What was the point? She couldn't undo what was done. And what was done was in fact done: Christopher O. Battle had made his exit from her life. Why dredge him up?

Because you can't help yourself.

Since his two-question telephone call, she'd tried to restore her life to its pre-Battle sense of order and purpose. But little things refused to revert to normal. She'd started to read his column during her first cup of coffee instead of her second—and sometimes before she'd even gotten the paper inside. She checked her message machine with a certain breathlessness and emerged from her laps in the hotel pool with her myopic eyes squinting, just in case. She even lingered as she passed security guards, half expecting them to tell her they'd tossed the louse again. She was preoccupied with Chris Battle. Obsessed. Yet her practical nature told her she ought to be proud of herself for getting him to withdraw from her life, *and* it told her that was exactly what he had done and she should forget him.

But she couldn't.

And so she'd called William Norton and now was on her way over to his office, not knowing precisely what she was getting herself into, which wasn't like Page B. Harrington at all.

William's secretary told her to go right into his office. She did. William looked up from his desk and shook his head miserably and he said, "Oh, Page . . . I feel so *guilty*."

"And well you should."

"You're not going to let me off the hook, huh?"

"I trusted you, William. Did you know he was planning to do a column on me? Did you owe him a favor, did he bribe you, were you angry with me?"

"No, yes, yes, and no, of course not."

Page blinked and digested his answers, having forgotten, at least momentarily, that William Norton wasn't an easy man to figure. A true eccentric, which made helping him organize himself more than an ordinary challenge. She should have known *instantly* that he was the traitor.

"What was the bribe?"

"Celtics tickets—for the memo." He twitched uncomfortably in his chair and scratched behind his ear with the eraser end of his pencil. "And, uh, well, I also let him bribe me about this afternoon."

Page frowned, and her pulse quickened. "What about this afternoon?"

"I told him you found out about me, and he said you'd be disappointed if he didn't show."

"And you *believed* him!"

"Well, no, not exactly, but he— God, Page, I really do feel guilty."

She regarded her former client with open suspicion, but she couldn't deny the excitement that gripped her. "'Fess up, William."

"I told him you were on your way over," he said haltingly, "and I agreed—"

"You *what*?"

"Hello, Page B."

Chris Battle's rich voice was like a warm, heavy liquid on her spine. As she turned, she took in everything in one swift glance—his beat-up running shoes, his rugged twill pants, his blue chambray shirt rolled up to just below his elbows, his tanned, hairy forearms, his strong neck, his stubborn jaw, his narrowed slate eyes and his tousled dark hair. There was nothing extraordinary about his looks—except, perhaps, the extraordinary effect they had on her. She herself was dressed in a classic but smart navy suit. Before stepping into William's trendy building, she'd carefully wiped the spring mud off her shoes. Chris Battle hadn't bothered.

"Good afternoon," she said stiffly, before flying back around at William, who'd slunk down in his chair and had begun unwinding a paper clip. She inhaled and said scathingly on the exhale, "*Well?* How did he get you to sell me out this time?"

William looked miserable. "Bruins tickets."

"Your thirty pieces of silver."

"Oh, come off it," Chris interrupted. "Why don't you make him feel worse than he already does?"

"I intend to! William, how could you? *Hockey* tickets—my God."

"They're seats behind the penalty box."

"I don't care if they're on the damn fifty-yard line!"

William cracked a meager smile. "No fifty-yard line in hockey, Page. You have two blue lines and a center red line—"

"I *know* there's no fifty-yard line. It was just an expression, and you are not going to get me off track. William, I trusted you."

"And I trust Chris. Page, we all have our breaking points—even you."

Chris laughed, sounding genuinely amused. "Page B. have a weakness? Perish the thought, my man. She's told you what the *B* stands for, hasn't she? Barracuda. Page Barracuda Harrington. If a barracuda has a weakness, I don't want to go through all the trouble of finding out what it is. Might get my hand bitten off."

Page groaned. *"Enough!"*

As she flew around, she wished she had long, wild hair so it could whip into her face and make her look even more ferocious. But she didn't. Her short, neat hair stayed in place. "Hockey tickets," she said with a derisive snort, glaring at Chris. She hated being betrayed, but her anger was more a pretense than a reality. It helped disguise the rush of excitement—or pure energy—that she felt at seeing Chris again. "Well, you're here. Now what?"

He gave her a disarming grin. "Coffee?"

The man certainly knew how to deflate her anger. Out of the corner of her eye she caught William, the rat, holding back a smirk. She recalled he wasn't married and, feeling vengeful, thought of Millie. She imagined her and William together and had to smile. Yes, indeed. Millie owed her one—owed her more than one, in fact. Revenge might be a waste of time, but there were those moments when it could be ever so sweet.

"Meet me at Rebecca's Café in five minutes," she told Chris, adding ominously, "I want to finish with William first."

"Sounds as if you plan to cut off a few of his fingers," Chris said with ill-timed amusement. "I'll wait outside for two minutes, and we'll go together. William, if I hear a scream, I'll race right in here to your rescue."

"Small comfort," William mumbled.

Page said innocently, "Don't you trust me to meet you?"

Chris laughed. "Nope, not a chance."

She supposed that in his position she would do the same. Five minutes to herself and she might just chuck the whole business and head back to her office and file papers. Or jump on the subway and go straight to Logan Airport and the nearest ticket counter. She could go to Paris. Spring in Paris sounded delightful.

But not as energizing, she had to admit, as coffee with Christopher O. Battle. She hadn't felt so . . . so alive in weeks.

"All right," she said. "Give me two minutes."

Battle swaggered out—it *was* a swagger, too—and Page folded her arms under her breasts and faced William as she might a rebellious eight-year-old. "So I'm not even worth the sacrifice of a couple of Bruins tickets."

"Page, Page, not many are, but *you*—definitely you are. Honestly. I'd never have given him the okay except for— Never mind. I've got a meeting."

"Except for what, William?"

"Nothing."

"Tell me. I think I have a right to know why people I consider my friends would accept hockey and basketball tickets as bribes from someone who's obviously out to get me."

"That's just it, Page."

"I beg your pardon?"

William looked as if he'd regretted even opening his mouth, but he went ahead, "Chris and you— Lord, you're meant for each other. You know my forte is putting together the unexpected. Well, that's what you two are. Unexpected. But you're so damn organized that you'd likely have organized yourself right out of any chance with this guy if I hadn't . . . well, allowed myself to be bribed. I'd have done something, anyway, once I found out Chris was after you. The tickets were just an added incentive." He sighed, shaking his head, an expression of warmth and friendship on his face. "Page, look at you. You backed yourself into such a corner that unless someone acted—namely me—you could very well have let Battle slip right by."

"William, you're not making any sense."

"Tell me that in two months."

She scowled, not willing to get serious about backing herself into a corner and Chris Battle being perfect for her. She couldn't get serious about such things, because then she'd have to examine the potential consequences and . . .

Well, it was best to maintain what Millie would no doubt call her schoolgirl attitude. She told William, "You just don't want me chopping off your fingers."

He laughed a little nervously. "Oh, that's just Chris talking. I know you wouldn't resort to violence."

But Millie Friedenbach she would resort to. "When's the hockey game?"

"Tonight." William was having difficulty looking sheepish.

"Got anyone to go with?"

"I'm working on it. I've got a couple of buddies I can call."

"As it so happens, William, I have a friend who loves hockey—a woman."

"Oh, yeah?"

"Uh-huh. Tall, blond, willowy."

"Do I know her?"

"I doubt it. Her name's Millie Friedenbach." *She's strong as an ox and if you get out of line with her, well, one simply didn't.* "Here, I'll give you her number." She jotted it down on the calendar she'd suggested he purchase. "Call her."

William beamed. "I will. Thanks, Page. I'm glad there're no hard feelings."

"None whatsoever."

Chris poked his head back in the office. "Your two minutes are up."

She gave him a look filled with challenge. "Going to club me and haul me off on your shoulder?"

"Who needs a club?" he said, and started toward her.

"All *right*." She turned once more to William. "Don't forget Millie."

"I won't."

"And I'll—"

But Battle grabbed her wrist, and what she did was get out the door and follow him onto Newbury Street.

A TINY BRANCH of the much larger Rebecca's on Charles Street, the Rebecca's on Newbury Street wasn't crowded. The menu—mostly soups and sandwiches and irresistible sweets—was written on blackboards behind the glass counters, and with the limited seating everything was available to go. Given the gorgeous weather, most people had taken their food outside. But Page and Chris ordered large coffees and sat at a small table in the dark, windowless rear of the café. At this point, Page thought, sunshine seemed relatively unimportant.

Chris sipped the very hot coffee and studied Page over the rim of the paper cup in a manner that made it impossible for her to look away. He said, "You're not really mad, are you?"

"At whom—you or William?"

"Both."

She shrugged in an attempt to appear cool and clinical, exactly the opposite of how she felt. How had she managed two weeks without this kind of interplay? She sighed. "Who can stay mad at William? He's like a big teddy bear—but talented, I'll warrant. He's also your friend and has been, I gather, for some time. His loyalty to you would be greater than to me."

Chris's eyes danced. "Do you analyze everything?"

"I'm just trying to give a complete answer." She spoke calmly, refusing to let him get to her, and dumped two half-and-halfs into her coffee. "As for you, I must say it's interesting to have someone so determined to get to me that he'll give up prized Celtics and Bruins tickets. That's never happened to me before. It's not easy to stay angry when one's experiencing something new."

Chris scowled. "So that's what I am—a new experience?"

"Well, I've never met anyone like you before."

She hadn't meant her voice to sound like that, so deep, almost sultry, almost flirtatious. She decided to blame the warm breeze that had floated in as the door opened and closed, letting in a steady stream of people. Analyzing her anger was relatively safe—it made it easier to keep her distance—but analyzing her reaction to Chris Battle didn't seem safe at all.

He seemed to sense her discomfort and, instead of pouncing, smiled. "Ditto for me as far as you're concerned."

"Does that mean you've decided not to do your column on professional organizers?"

"Yeah. I gave myself two weeks to quit thinking about wanting to kiss you, and you know what?" He set down his coffee and hooked one arm over the back of the chair, his eyes lost in the shadows of the dark corner where their table was. His mouth twitched; he seemed so at ease with himself and with her. "It didn't work."

"I see." She didn't know what else to say.

"Page B., I hate to tell you, but you don't see at all." He fished in his jacket pocket and produced what appeared to be two burned matches and placed them in the center of the table. "Here."

"What's that?" she asked.

He said, "Two burned matches."

"That's what I thought. Do they have any significance?"

"Yeah, they have a lot of significance. They're what I used to burn all the notes I took on you, your clients, your work, all my aborted drafts, everything. I burned it all. I was going to bring you the ashes but—" he unhooked his arm from the back of his chair and picked up his coffee cup "—too messy."

She picked up one of the charred matches and watched the tip break off, crumbling. "You're giving up?"

"Quitting. It's different from giving up. Page B., if I wanted to pursue this story, I would—and nothing you did would stop me."

"You'd just be spinning your wheels, Christopher O.," she said, mimicking him. "But never mind. Of all things, I wouldn't have pegged you as someone who'd quit."

"I made a conscious ethical decision after taking an honest look at all the facts and feelings involved with this piece."

"Meaning?"

He smiled. "Don't you understand your own kind of pompous-ass mumbo jumbo? What I mean is simply that I can't in good conscience write about you. I'm not sure I believe there's such a thing as objectivity—we all state our convictions from within our convictions, as some philosopher once said. But a journalist still has to maintain at least some sense of objectivity."

"You're a columnist," she pointed out. "You're never objective. You let people have it all the time."

"Yes, but I let them cook their own gooses. I don't cook them for them. I try to go at my stories from as objective a standpoint as I can." He paused and gave her a long look, adding, "I don't write about my friends."

"Never?"

"Never."

"I suppose that's commendable."

He laughed. "I haven't heard that word since my second-grade teacher congratulated me for writing my name so she could read it. Commendable or not, that's the code I operate under. No columns about friends or ex-wives or women I've gone to bed with—or want to go to bed with."

His look was direct and honest and made Page want to run because she knew she wasn't a friend or an ex-wife or a woman who had ever been to bed with him. That only left a woman he wanted to go to bed with, which was in another ballpark altogether from just being a woman he felt like kissing.

"Forget it," she said.

"Hmm?"

"I don't believe you."

"Meaning you don't believe what I'm saying, or you don't believe I'm saying what I'm saying?"

He was having a damn good time. Too good. She went on crisply. "Meaning I don't believe you burned your notes or anything resembling your notes. Meaning I'm not your friend, I'm not your ex-wife, I'm not a woman you've been to bed with and I'm not a woman you have any desire of going to bed with. Meaning, in short, that *I* think this is just another of your ploys to get into my office so you can do your article."

She didn't get to him, not at all. He drank some coffee and shook his head. "You just don't want to admit it."

"Admit *what*?"

"That you're attracted to me just as much as I am to you." His gaze leveled on her in such a way she couldn't bring herself to turn away. "You, Ms Organizer, have had thoughts about going to bed with me, and don't you deny it."

She inhaled deeply. "I refuse to discuss such matters in . . . in a business setting."

"Don't go priggish on me. Look, we've gotten off to a bad start, I'll admit. So take the two matches and consider this a new beginning—a truce, even. Forget I ever thought professional organizers were silly or sleazy. Forget I ever figured I'd stick it to you good in my colunn. Forget the whole mess. Okay? We'll start over."

"It's not working."

He sighed. "You don't trust me, do you?"

"How perceptive of you."

"Well, I guess I can't blame you. Want to go back to my apartment and see my pile of ashes?"

She didn't hesitate for a second. "Yes."

She didn't think his swallow of coffee went down too well. "You're serious?"

"Damn right."

"You're willing to be alone with me in my apartment even after I've told you I have designs on your body?"

"Sure. You've said yourself—and to some degree proved—that brutishness isn't your style. Lying and cheating and sneaking around, yes. But not brutishness. When it really counts, you'll take no for an answer. So, Mr. Battle, shall we?" She grinned at him, *knowing* she had him. *Ashes my hind end*, she thought. "I'd love to see your ashes."

THEY WALKED UP NEWBURY and, instead of taking one of the meandering paths through the Public Garden, cut directly down Arlington and crossed over to Beacon Street. Chris wasn't once tempted to take Page B. Harrington's hand and swing it. She'd probably bite his wrist off. She was in just that kind of mood. He couldn't blame her, but did she have to be so damn thorough?

Out of the corner of one eye, while pretending to be completely at ease with the situation, he studied her and wondered how he'd lasted two weeks without seeing her. At night he'd sat at his desk and seen the light in her window across the Garden, and imagined her sitting there, looking for the light in his attic window. Did she ever daydream? Did she ever acknowledge that it was far, far more than a simple waste of time? Somehow, he thought so. There was a sensitive woman beneath all that starch and vinegar. He admired her competence and intelligence, but he wanted to dig deeper and find out what else was there. He wanted to hear her tell him her hopes and her dreams as she lay in his arms.

Fat chance, he thought dismally.

Making love to her seemed such a hopeless longing on his part. They were so different, Page and him. If only it were just her turquoise eyes and trim shape that he found so attractive. But he also was drawn to her laugh and her quick wit and her smart-aleckness and her concern for others . . . and her mystery. What made her tick was as big a question now as it had been weeks ago. Only now he wanted to know for his own sake, not his column's.

But what the hell. He was doomed, anyway.

There were no ashes.

He hadn't burned his notes. He hadn't burned a thing. What self-respecting reporter would? The matches *had* been a ploy.

"You bastard," he muttered to himself as they turned up Beacon.

He was every bit as bad as Page thought he was. No, the matches hadn't been a ploy to get into her apartment so he could do his column. But they'd still been a ploy—to get on her good side the easy way, with none of the hard work. That accomplished, they could go on and be friends, then lovers.

In Page's world view, however, ploys were lies, and lies weren't tolerated.

And she'd already revealed herself to be anything but forgiving.

What was more, he hadn't *exactly* abandoned the article—or not abandoned it, either. He'd tried a number of times to write the damn thing, just to exorcise Page from his thoughts once and for all. But images of her would interfere. In incredible detail he could see her lovely, pale-skinned body climbing from the hotel pool, her bright smile and her turquoise eyes sparkling with anger and determination. He'd thought coffee with her might help him to decide, one way or the other, what to do about her. He *knew* he couldn't do the column. He really did. But how was he going to convince Page she hadn't been conned?

The truth was out, at least for the moment. She'd be too angry to hear the subtle distinctions he would have to make for her to understand his complicated motivations. What he had to do, he reasoned, was come up with some ashes—preferably not his own.

6

PAGE LEANED AGAINST the wall in the lobby of Chris's building as he fished out his keys. She noticed this time he didn't bother with any pretense of not being able to find them. He stuck the key in the door and grinned at her, as if he knew what she was thinking. She smiled back. She doubted it was much of a smile. As she'd walked along beside him, she'd had a curious urge to scoop up his hand, swing his arm and run with him. It was madness, of course. But any more mad than going up to his apartment to see his ashes?

"Chickening out?" he asked, his look filled with challenge and amusement.

"Of course not."

"Not Page B. Once you've made up your mind, that's it."

"Exactly."

"You're one tough lady, right?"

"That depends on what you mean by 'tough.' As I've already indicated, Mr. Battle, you don't scare me."

He laughed as he pushed the door open with his shoulder. "I'm onto you, sweetheart. Whenever I strike a nerve, you start with the 'Mr. Battle' routine. You *are* thinking about chickening out."

She was. She wasn't going to admit it to him, but she was reconsidering, trying to make herself reconsider. Chickening out seemed to be a wise course of action, although not because she was afraid of him. She was simply ill at ease with her mixed feelings toward him. Spring fever seemed to have gotten hold of her sensible nature, and who knew what would happen next. Already she was noticing too much about him. In the sunlight she'd spotted touches of gray in his stubble of beard and the slight glisten of perspiration on his brow. She'd observed the wrinkles in his shirt, its cotton fabric worn and soft with use, making him seem even sexier, and her gaze had dwelled for seconds too long on the good-quality leather belt that had to be a decade old. He wasn't slick and polished and packaged. Like everything else, she'd noticed that about him, too.

What was more disconcerting, she'd reacted. Her response was in no way professional or distanced or that of the wronged target of a relentless journalist. Walking beside him, she'd wanted him to touch her. Her lips tingled with the urge to touch his. Her fingertips itched with the need to reach out and feel a part of him, any part, hands, hair, face, stomach, thighs. Her spine ached with a longing so deep, so basic that she had almost groaned aloud. If it was only spring fever, it was the worse case she'd ever had!

But he was still Christopher O. Battle, still relentless, still unpredictable, still a liar. Still unsuitable. Still not the man for her. She had fought too long and too hard for some stability in her life, and she wasn't going to lose it, not for him, not for anyone.

"I am *not* chickening out," she said firmly, and swept through the door after him.

"You're sure?" he asked.

There was something tentative in his voice that, preoccupied with her own ambivalence, she hadn't noticed before. She eyed him suspiciously. "Do you *want* me to chicken out?"

He shrugged unconvincingly. "Makes no difference to me."

Interesting, she thought. Interesting, indeed. She prided herself on her judgment of character. In her business such a skill was critical. Any journalist burning his notes would raise her eyebrows. Journalists simply didn't do such things. But a tenacious, hard-hitting, cynical columnist like Chris Battle burning his notes seemed very much on the incredible side. In fact, unbelievable. Taking on professional organizers wasn't in the same league as taking on political corruption or the illegal dumping of hazardous chemicals, but Chris was a professional. He wouldn't make such distinctions, particularly while he was hot on the scent of whatever project consumed his interest.

Which meant it was highly unlikely he'd burned his notes.

Which meant he might or might not have abandoned his column on professional organizers.

Which meant he was a liar, and she had probably been conned.

"That's good," she said, deciding to let him roast for a while in his own fire.

She followed him up the five flights of stairs and derived great satisfaction from watching a little more sweat break out on his brow. Inside his apartment everything was just as untidy as it had been a few weeks ago. The coat tree teetered when he tossed his jacket among the collection that had gathered there over the long winter.

"Some coffee?" he asked.

"No, thanks. Where are the ashes?"

He rubbed his stubble of beard. "I think I've misled you."

"Oh?"

"I didn't really burn the notes. It sounded dramatic and seemed like a fun thing to tell you, like something you'd swallow. A game, you know? So that's what I told you. As it happens, I didn't actually burn them. My building's old. Couldn't very well risk a fire, could I?"

She tucked her thumbs in the corners of her suit jacket pockets. "You lied."

"Yeah."

There was no remorse in his tone or his expression. His easy admission—as if to say what was the big deal—deflated her anger somewhat, but not anywhere near enough to compel her to retreat to Beacon Street.

"Why did you drag me all the way up here before telling me?" she demanded. "Why not admit you lied back in the café and save us both the trouble?"

He headed for his kitchen and grabbed an apple out of a mixing bowl on the table, offering it to her. She shook her head, and he bit into it. Something about the way he chewed rekindled the ache in her back, and she began to pace, hoping it would help. It didn't.

"I was hoping I could come up with a good cover on the way over," he said.

"You mean another lie?"

"If you want to be so bald about it, yes, another lie."

"But you couldn't come up with one?"

"Didn't."

She snorted. "What kind of cover could you have come up with? Either you have ashes, or you don't have ashes!"

He swallowed a chunk of his apple, still not looking contrite. "I considered telling you I'd sprinkled them on the Public Garden so we could both think about my sacrifice whenever we looked out our windows." He spoke in a mockingly mournful voice, as if the ashes were those of a deceased mutual friend, not some damn notes. "I was even going to show you the exact spot where the ashes of my hard work had met the dirt and mud of—"

"Oh, spare me. I'd never have swallowed that!"

A small, unrepentant smile escaped. "No? You swallowed the line about the ashes in the first place. Two burned matches—and you the Ms Organized Barracuda. Gullible, gullible."

"Don't turn this back around to me, Battle. *You're* the one who lied."

"And you're the one who fell for it." He winked at her and took another chomp of apple.

"That hardly makes us even."

"Who's keeping score?"

"I am."

"Page, let's talk."

But she refused to hear him as she flounced over to his desk and began madly flipping through the piles of papers. "Where are the notes?" she asked, feeling breathless and wild. "You didn't dispose of them at all, did you?"

"Now wait just a minute." He was behind her in an instant. "Nobody touches my desk."

"I shouldn't imagine anyone would want to."

He grabbed her wrist as she reached for a folder and pulled her around toward him. She didn't fight him. She didn't want to, couldn't. She knew what was coming, and her fears and inhibitions no longer mattered.

"I can't stand this," she whispered, her gaze locking with his.

"Neither can I."

His voice was husky and rich and honest. He had her wrist up by her throat, an awkward but not painful position, and let his hand move slowly down her forearm to her crooked elbow, which was pressed against her breast. Then he skipped from her elbow to her ribs, the knuckles of his thumb just skimming the lower part of her breast as she moved not away from him, but toward him. His eyes never left hers. His lips were parted slightly, and her mind spun with images of what they'd feel like on her mouth, her nipples, her—

You can't do this!

She turned sharply, and his hand fell away. "Look at this," she said, her voice strained, the laugh that was supposed to have been caustic a pathetic sound. "It's unbelievable. Grocery lists in among your business notes, phone messages scrawled on anything available, scraps of paper that may or not be anything worth saving, tear sheets just tossed any ol' place, clippings—"

"Page, don't." His voice was soft, a caress.

"Look here—a birthday card for your mother."

"What? So there it is. I was wondering what happened to it. Hey, now I'm only a week late." He smiled as her eyes met his. "There, I knew that'd get you to look at me."

Her throat was dry and tight, but she maintained her "Ms Organizer" facade. "How you get anything done is completely beyond me."

"How doesn't matter. That I do should be enough."

He spoke quietly and smiled again, a soft, tender smile that lit up his eyes and made him look more than roguishly sexy, more than simply a man wanting a quick and meaningless toss in bed. She felt jittery and silly. It was so much easier just to keep their animosity going.

"I . . . I think your honesty unnerves me more than your dishonesty," she said, then turned away quickly and snatched up a book of matches. "What's this? If you don't smoke, I don't understand—" She'd opened the matchbook and spotted her phone number on the inside flap. "Oh, I see. Well, luckily there's a whole book of matches here. That should suffice to get us a nice fire going. Where are the notes on professional organizers?"

"Page," Chris said, curiously calm, "I'm not going to let you burn my notes."

"Then you admit you didn't get rid of them?"

"Look around and see for yourself. I'm a pack rat. I never get rid of anything."

"Least of all notes for a potential column."

"It's not a potential column. I'm not going to do it. I'm sorry I lied, Page. I'm sorry we've gotten off to such a rotten start. I'm sorry I'm not such an easy guy to trust. But if you've never believed anything I've told you, believe me now. I'm not going to do that piece."

She turned around to face him and leaned against the desk. "Why are you being nice?"

"I have to have an ulterior motive?"

"Not 'have to.' But you probably do."

He smiled. "If I'm not nice, you won't talk to me and explain why you pulled away from me a minute ago."

"What you should be asking is why I didn't pull away sooner."

"Okay. Why didn't you?"

"Spring fever."

"Why don't you trust your own emotions?"

"Because . . ." No, she couldn't explain. She couldn't even begin to explain. And even if she could, she wasn't sure she wanted to. Chris Battle was attracted to a combative, give-as-good-as-she-gets woman. She wasn't going to expose her weaknesses. "It's not important. Chris, I want you to do your column on professional organizers."

He didn't say a word, just regarded her with his infamous skepticism.

"Don't you want to know why I've changed my mind?" she asked.

"I think it's fairly obvious. You want to keep hating me, and the column will help. That way you don't have to confront your feelings."

"No, not at all." She tried to sound crisp and businesslike, but instead sounded shocked, even hurt. Had she been that big a jerk that he thought she hated him? "It seems to me that you think with pen in hand. You gather information and process it through your writing. You've been gathering information on me and what I do, but in order for you to make sense of any of it, you've got to write. So write. Do the column." She looked away. "Understand me."

She was relieved when he didn't tell her she wasn't making any sense and didn't try to touch her, because this time she wouldn't have pulled away. Even with what little she'd said, she'd never opened herself up in such a way as to invite probing, understanding. It was safer to remain a mystery.

"I'll need to see your office," he said.

"Nine o'clock tomorrow morning."

He smiled, but she could see the confusion in his eyes. "Sharp?"

She grinned back. "Of course."

He leaned against his desk and watched her as she told him goodbye and left, moving faster as she hit the landing outside the apartment and even faster as she hit the stairs. She took them two at a time. Outside she leaped down his front stoop and stumbled, twisting her ankle, but she righted herself immediately. She knew Battle was up there watching her. She could feel his eyes on her.

"Hey, Page B."

She looked up in the sunlight and saw his head thrust out of his attic window. Saw his grin.

"What'd you do with that birthday card?"

"I didn't do anything with it. *You* took it."

"I did?"

She groaned. "Yes."

"Well, it's around here somewhere. Your ankle okay?"

"It's fine."

"See? You need me."

"How do you figure?"

His grin broadened. "The irritation factor. I keep you on edge."

That he did. His head disappeared back inside, and the window shut with a thud. Page headed up Beacon and ducked quickly onto Charles Street, out of view of

Chris's attic. Then she found an ice-cream shop and bought herself a cup of raspberry sorbet.

Spring, she thought miserably. Would she survive it?

AT NINE O'CLOCK the next morning Chris still wasn't dressed. He lay flat on his back on his bed, stark naked, and contemplated his bedroom ceiling. No coffee stains there, but the white plaster, almost gray now, needed painting. There were a few cracks that could use patching. When he made love to Page, she'd probably comment on the state of his ceiling.

He shut his eyes and groaned. "My man, that's not funny."

But in an odd, painful way, it summed up his confusion. He had lain awake most of the night wondering what the hell was going on between him and the unexpectedly unpredictable organizer. Was he doing the column? No, no way. He couldn't. At the very least, it'd be unethical. So why had he agreed to show up this morning? Because he wanted to know more about her, and it seemed a good way to get at the inner workings of Page B. Harrington. But also a dishonest way. Which was why he wasn't dressed.

He supposed Page was fuming by now. He should call, but what would he say? *I'm not coming.* But he might. *I'll be late.* But he already was, and he hadn't decided he would in fact go. *I want to see you, but not on business.* She'd tell him not to bother; *she* wasn't going to waste a morning's work. *I'm lying here in bed wishing you were here with me.* For sure she'd tell him not to come.

The course of least resistance was just to get dressed and get moving.

But when he arrived at the Four Seasons, one of his security guard buddies handed him an envelope. Inside he found a key and a note printed on Get It Together Inc. stationery.

I don't know if you're just late because you're irresponsible and inconsiderate, or if *you* chickened out and aren't coming. I don't even care. If you get here, here's the key to my apartment. Go on in and have yourself a ball. I have a 10:30 meeting and won't be back until 4:15.

Sincerely,
Page Harrington

He loved the "sincerely." From the looks of her handwriting—she'd practically punched holes in the paper she'd pressed so hard—he guessed she'd have liked to send him off with a less professional closure, something in the vein of "rot in hell."

Inconsiderate and irresponsible, was he? From her point of view, maybe. From his, he had simply tried to spare her feelings—and his own, too, he supposed. Would she have rather he'd called her and told her he was lying in bed naked thinking about making love to her?

What the hell. He scrawled *that* on the back of her note, tucked it back in its envelope and returned it and the key to the security guard.

"Wait," he said. "On second thought, I'll take the key."

No point in burning all his bridges.

I didn't call you because I was lying in bed naked thinking about making love to you and didn't want to embarrass you.

Page felt a curious thrill when she read Chris's note as she rode the elevator up to her condominium. Was he serious?

She snorted in self-disgust. "What difference does it make if he is?"

She crumpled the note and shoved it in her handbag.

She'd fumed all day. *All* day. She'd permitted her anger at being stood up to dominate her thoughts. She'd wondered if he'd showed up after all, just late. She'd debated calling her apartment to see if he was there. She'd considered calling his apartment to find out what had happened to him. She'd thought up a host of new names to call him.

In short, she'd stewed.

But she'd felt an electric current coiling up her spine as she'd deciphered his handwriting. More games? Again, she thought, what difference did it make? Despite her stewing, she had been able to take a cold clinical look at the facts—or at least *the* fact, the one she could no longer ignore: Christopher O. Battle was a threat to her hard-won stability. Not a potential threat, but an actual threat. Who was more at fault or who wanted to go to bed with whom were no longer the salient points.

She had to regain control over her own life.

There was no sign that he'd been inside her apartment. No footprints on the rug, no coffee mug in the sink, no forgotten jacket or scrap of paper. Nor was there a message from her on her machine. All she had was the note. She dug it out of her handbag and read it again, just to be sure she'd gotten it right.

I didn't call you because I was lying in bed naked thinking about making love to you and didn't want to embarrass you.

She picked up the phone and called him.

"Battle," he said after five rings.

"Did you know it was me and not want to pick up the phone?"

"Naw. Couldn't find the phone. I dumped it on the floor so I could spread out my research on a new column I'm working on. Did you get my note?"

"What note?"

"You lie, Page. You lie poorly, I might add, but you do lie."

How could a man so completely her opposite see through her so easily? She flipped the note over so she didn't have to look at his provocative scrawl. "I don't know what you're talking about. The envelope I gave the security guard didn't have the key in it and he said he'd given it to you. So I just threw my old note away. You'd written a note to me on it?"

"Uh-huh."

"What did it say? Anything important?"

"Don't bait me, Page B. It won't work."

Maybe not, but she did love baiting him. She could feel herself beginning to smile, energy coursing through her after her day of fuming. "Well, I suppose it's neither here nor there. Did you come upstairs and have your look around?"

"Nope."

"Why not?"

"No fun if you're not there."

"But you've seen me. It's my office you need to see now to complete your column."

"None of this has anything to do with my column, and you damn well know it."

"But—"

"Give me an hour to finish up here. You and I are having dinner together tonight. If you haven't read the note, dig it out of the trash and read it. If you have, read it again. You and I are going to talk."

"Look here, who died and made you boss? You stood me up this morning, and I'm not going to sit around for another hour waiting for you to show up."

"I'll be there, Page. Count on it."

"No, that's the whole point. I'm not going to put myself in the position of having to count on you and—" She took a breath and abandoned her explanation. "Just don't come."

She hung up, banging down the receiver as hard as she could.

Ten seconds later her phone rang. She let her message machine take care of it. Chris Battle's rich, sexy voice said, "Page B., did you forget? I have a key."

She dove for the phone, but he'd already hung up.

It was 4:35. If he wasn't there by 5:35, she would go stay with Millie Friedenbach for a few days and have all her locks changed. To Chris Battle, being late or not showing up might not mean much. To her, it was a symbol of irresponsibility, disorganization, selfishness, laziness—and just not caring. Good intentions meant something, but not enough.

Thoughts of Millie reminded her of last night's Bruins game and William Norton. Glad for the diversion, Page called her friend.

"Hey, there, friend," Millie said, laughing, "I've been meaning to phone you all day. Thanks for putting William Norton onto me. What a sweetie he is. We're having dinner tonight, I think."

"You think?"

"Yeah, we're leaving it open. I'll give him a call in a few minutes and find out what's happening with his schedule. Maybe I'll get him to come to the gym with me. He's got a few pounds he could work off."

"But you like him?"

"Yeah, he's a nice guy."

"And he likes you?"

"Seems to."

So much for revenge, Page thought. Not that she'd owed Millie a bad night, but Millie Friedenbach had been known to do nearly anything to get free hockey tickets.

Millie went on. "It's refreshing to meet a guy who doesn't get all weird when he finds out I know as much about hockey and stuff as he does."

"He's a friend of Chris Battle."

"Yes, dearie, I know. And as far as I'm concerned, it's a point in William's favor. What're you and Battle up to?"

"We're having dinner tonight . . . I think."

"Relax, Page. Be spontaneous for a change and go with the flow."

"I'm not even sure he'll show up."

"How long's he got?"

She glanced at the clock. "Forty-seven minutes."

"Hey, be bold and give him fifty."

"Millie—"

"I'm not making fun of you, Page. I just don't want you to wreck a potentially good thing here. William thinks Chris has 'romantic inclinations' toward you— you believe he actually talks like that? Don't be so picky, all right? I mean, who'd have ever thought I'd be smitten by a guy with a mushy middle? If there is such a thing as Mr. Right, I wouldn't want to meet him. Life would be boring."

And with that shaky philosophical pronouncement, Millie wished Page a good night.

During the next forty minutes Page took a quick shower, dabbed on a light perfume and changed into a pink knit dress. She took pains with her cosmetics to make her face appear natural; she wasn't the sort of woman who could just slap on eyeliner and lip gloss and look fantastic. As with most things, she took great care in choosing the right look for her pale skin and deeper colored hair, which, fortunately, required two minutes of work. Her contact lenses were feeling glued in, so she took them out and put on her pink-framed glasses. All in all, she thought, examining herself in the full-length mirror, not bad. Not free-spirited, not funky, but not uptight, either.

So you're dressing up for this guy, is that it?

"Yes," she said aloud, "I guess it is."

But since he wasn't going to show up, anyway, why worry?

At precisely 5:35 her doorbell rang. She couldn't believe it, but when she looked through her peephole, there was Chris. She opened the door.

He grinned. "I've been out here for five minutes, but I wanted to show up on the dot. Here." He thrust a bouquet of spring flowers at her.

"What's this?" she asked.

"Flowers—daffodils, irises, couple of tulips. I don't know what that frothy stuff is. Some kind of filler, I guess."

"Baby's breath. But why?"

"For being a jerk."

She laughed. "I've never received flowers for being a jerk."

She saw surprise reach his eyes, and then he smiled at her, and she let him inside. They went to the kitchen, where Page got out a vase. Chris watched from the doorway as she filled the vase with water, snipped off the ends of the flowers and added them. She set the arrangement on her small kitchen table.

"Very nice," she said, meaning it. "Thank you."

"You're welcome. You dressed up for dinner?"

"Not really."

He moved into the kitchen toward her. "Why is it you can lie freely to me, but when I lie to you, all hell breaks loose?"

She shrugged. "I don't know. Because you don't have as hot a temper as I do?"

"Don't count on it."

"Then because your lies are important and mine are . . . defensive. To keep you at a distance."

"Is that what you want? Me at a distance?"

He was standing very close. She'd turned to face the flowers and had her back to him but could hear his footfall directly behind her. He'd lowered his voice, and she could almost feel his breath on her neck. Or maybe not almost. Maybe she actually could, and she just didn't want to admit it.

"Part of me says I should," she said, not turning.

"Because of the column?"

"No. Not at all. I believe you when you say you're not going to do it. It'd be unethical. Whatever anyone's said about you, you've never been accused of being unethical. Wrongheaded, cynical, nasty, mean spirited, tough—"

"But not unethical. Is that a compliment?"

Now she did turn, and he was even closer than she'd imagined. Close enough to brush up against. Close enough, in fact, that she had no other choice. She lost her balance for an instant, nearly tripping over his feet, but caught him by the arm and steadied herself. Her gaze locked with his, and she nodded. "Yes," she said, "it is."

"But it's not really the column standing between us," he said.

It wasn't a question, but she shook her head. "It's difficult to explain."

"Will you try?"

There was a sensitivity in his expression, a desire to understand that she hadn't seen before. With one finger he brushed a bit of flower from the shoulder of her dress. His touch, ever so brief and unconscious, sent sensations radiating through her. She nodded. "Over dinner?"

"Sure. Where would you like to go?"

"I don't know. Let's just walk outside and see where we end up."

He grinned, a teasing grin, but one without ridicule and that touch of superiority she'd detected the first day they'd met. "How spontaneous, Ms Organizer."

She laughed. "Downright daring."

"There's one thing I've got to do first."

"Check out my office? It's color-coded, you know, and—"

"I don't give a damn about your office. It's this."

They were still standing close, and he scooped an arm around her waist and threw her balance off so that she stepped on his toes and catapulted against him. She had to swing both her arms around him to keep from falling, but apparently that had been the whole idea. She heard herself take a sharp breath as she felt the warmth and hardness of his body against hers. His arm stayed around her middle. She liked the weight of it on the small of her back, liked the way it helped to keep her pushed up against him.

"I've been wanting to hold you like this for *weeks*."

She gave a small, breathless laugh and tried to come up with something witty, something that wouldn't tell him the effect he was having on her. She said lightly, "The greatest rewards go to those who are patient."

"Who the hell says I've been patient?"

He wrapped his other arm around her, and they snuggled even closer. She loved the smells of him—no-nonsense soap and hard work—and could have stayed in his arms for the rest of the evening.

"No," he said, bringing his mouth toward hers, "patience has nothing to do with it."

He touched her lips briefly with his, as if trying to make it enough but already knowing it wouldn't be. He was also giving her that instant to pull back. But she didn't. She opened her mouth in invitation, and his mouth seized hers, his tongue plunging in at once, its every movement, its sheer heat, betraying the same kind of ache that overwhelmed her.

His fingers dug erotically into her buttocks, and he moaned softly as he pressed her against him. She could feel just how aroused he was and felt a stab of panic. She pulled back from the kiss. "Chris...Chris, are you sure this is making you feel better?"

He smiled at her, his eyes half-closed. "The potential for feeling better is definitely there. You?"

"I'm . . . hungry."

"So I gathered," he said, deliberately misinterpreting her. But he didn't press his point as he dropped his hands from her hips and stood back. "Dinner?"

She nodded, relieved. "I'll get my coat. Tell me . . . if I hadn't let you in, would you have used your key?"

"Absolutely."

"Isn't that unethical?"

"Work and romance have different sets of rules, Page B. There's not much I wouldn't do for work. But for romance . . . hell, who knows what I won't do?"

7

THE WARM EVENING, by Boston standards, had lured a sizable portion of the population out onto the streets and into the restaurants, which were very crowded. Chris and Page had to wait in line at the inexpensive no-frills side to Legal Seafoods, but Chris didn't mind. People were in the kind of giddy mood that came with the first days of spring after a long, cold winter. He decided that was something people in the Sun Belt missed: that inexplicable, overwhelming pleasure—the sheer *relief*—at hearing the first robin, seeing the first crocus, feeling the first breath of warm air. To experience that thrill was enough reason to endure winter, except, of course, for those couple of weeks he liked to spend in Jamaica.

The wait in line also gave him a chance to clear his head, and Page to clear hers. He sensed she was as caught up in the feverish emotions of spring as he was. They talked about things that didn't matter too much, such as whether they'd eat shark—Page would, he wouldn't—and sushi. "If it blinks," he maintained, "it gets cooked." That led to a discussion of what animals didn't blink—were there any?—and if he'd eat them raw, until Chris finally told Page not to be such a perfectionist.

"You know what I meant," he said.

"Well, yes, but you're a journalist, right? I should think you'd want to be precise about language."

"I am just making idle talk while waiting in line for dinner. Don't you believe in idle talk?"

"Sometimes."

He knew he was in for a lecture and watched her with amusement as she geared up.

"Actually," she said, "you'd be surprised at all you can accomplish while waiting in lines. Many of my clients can't stand waiting, but it's a fact of urban life. Instead of becoming frustrated, I suggest they use the time to empty their minds and relax, to observe people, to read a magazine, even to problem solve. The trick is not to focus on having to wait."

"You have a system for everything?"

"No, but I guess it might seem like that."

"It does. Anyway, that's what we're doing now—not focusing on having to wait."

She nodded. "Right."

"Then we agree?"

"That this is an idle conversation designed to make the wait more bearable? Yes, definitely."

He laughed. "So who the hell cares if lobsters blink?"

"I don't. I'm just saying—"

"No, don't. You're arguing for the sake of arguing, which, I might add, is a waste of time."

"Not necessarily." She spoke airily, but he knew she was goading him and enjoying their pointless discussion as much as he was. "Arguing can be highly productive, even when there's no need or hope of victory. It sharpens one's communications and logic skills and—"

"And thank God we're next in line."

They sat at a table overlooking the street, Page's back to the window, and debated the specials, shark being among them. Page settled on simple broiled scrod, Chris on salmon, and they ordered a bottle of dry white wine. Chris noticed that between their kiss and her baiting him, most of her rich, burnished-looking lipstick had rubbed off. Her lips were full, and he liked the way she sometimes bit down on one side; it made him think of taking a nibble himself.

Their wine and a basket of crusty rolls arrived. Page broke a roll in half and skipped the butter. Chris shook his head at her as he slathered his roll with two pats of high-fat, cholesterol-rich, one-hundred-percent pure creamery butter. He figured what the hell, he was having heart-healthy fish for dinner, wasn't he? "Don't you have any vices?"

She surprised him by laughing. "An attraction to chocolate and—" She waved her fingers. "Never mind."

"You can't say never mind. It's not fair. Anybody who doesn't put butter on her rolls and color-codes her office and admits she has not one but *two* vices...well, I have to know."

"No, you don't."

"I'm a relentless journalist, remember?"

"Not tonight."

"I may not be on the job, but the personality traits are still there—curiosity, nosiness, an undauntable need to know, all of which, mind you, get worse when I sense someone's trying to avoid telling me something I ought to know. You don't want me to be unbearable all evening, do you?"

"I don't mind. You're naturally unbearable."

He was fairly sure she was teasing him, but with Page B. sometimes it wasn't easy to tell. But he persisted. "An attraction to chocolate and what?"

She bit into her roll, having to tear a little with her teeth to break off the crust. To Chris, it was very erotic. He had to look away for a second and focus on the flood of traffic on the wide street outside. When he looked back at her, she was concentrating hard on his question as she licked a few crumbs off her lower lip. Deadly. Chris almost forgot what the hell he'd asked.

"Unsuitable men," she said.

"An attraction to unsuitable men? You?"

"Yes, unfortunately. And apparently they have an attraction to me, as well."

"And that's a vice?"

"Most definitely."

"Exactly what's an unsuitable man?"

"Unsuitable men cross all economic, political and social lines."

"I'm sure they do. Are they messy?"

She narrowed her eyes at him over her roll. "You're making fun of me."

"Just asking a question."

"It's not an objective question."

"Who said I was trying to be objective?"

She sighed. "Messiness doesn't necessarily have anything to do with it. An unsuitable man can be someone who looks to me—or any woman—to sort out his life for him, to tell him what to do, how to live, to set goals for him. In short, to be a kind of mother to him."

"Sweetheart, I assure you, that's not me."

"I know it isn't. I'm talking in generalities. An unsuitable man can also be someone who runs directly counter to my goals, to the kind of life *I* want and need to lead."

"Ever hear of the word 'compromise'?"

"How can you compromise on your life's dreams?"

"You don't necessarily have to compromise on the goals, just on the tactics, how you achieve those goals."

"My goals have too much to do with how I achieve them. In other words, tactics are my goals."

"Huh?"

"I need stability. I need to *live* a certain way."

"Then all men are going to be unsuitable, Page. You're not going to find a mirror image of yourself, somebody who does everything exactly the way you do it. Don't you see that?"

"Of course. But it's not that simple."

"Nothing ever is," he said.

When she fell silent, Chris ate some of his own roll, giving her space. This didn't seem to be the moment to press her to clarify her thinking. But he wanted to. He could feel his heart pounding in his chest and the muscles tensing all over his body as he forced himself to keep his mouth shut. He was used to pushing—asking question after question, probing, digging—until he had everything clear and straight in his own mind. He couldn't do that with Page, not yet. His reasons had changed, but he still wanted to know what made Page B. Harrington tick. More than ever, he had to know.

But he didn't want to give her an excuse to tell him flat out he was "unsuitable." His silence, he realized, wasn't just to protect her; it was to protect himself, too.

After a few minutes she said, "I wonder if eels blink."

"*Page.*"

"Doesn't the idea of eating raw eel disgust you? I read somewhere that eel blood can be deadly poisonous and—"

"That's disgusting. Another word and I don't think I'll be able to choke down my salmon."

She smiled innocently. "Am I ruining your dinner?"

"That and changing the subject, yes."

Their dinners arrived, and she changed the subject again, to politics. Chris let it go. Only elusive targets for his column did he believe in badgering into talking, not women who had gotten into a place inside him that made him feel warm and full and ever so vulnerable. He listened to her discuss a pending state bill, pleased with her depth of knowledge on the subject and more than a little relieved that they agreed on the worthiness of the legislation. They'd already argued over lobster and eel eyes. He didn't think they needed to argue over politics.

"But I'm doing most of the talking," she pointed out as she polished off her second glass of wine.

"That's okay. I like to listen to you."

"I'm glad, but I've been thinking that I know very little about you. I know many of your views because I read your column. I know you're witty, nasty, irreverent, funny when I agree with you and infuriating when I don't. I know you're a pack rat and not terribly neat. I know you have at least two ex-wives and a mother who received this year's birthday card late. I know—"

"One ex-wife," he said, "and my mother always gets birthday cards from me late. But I always remember to call."

Page was shaking her head impatiently. "We'll get to your mother in a minute. What do you mean, one ex-wife?"

He tilted his glass back and finished his wine, studying the expression on Page's face. He could see the excitement there, the relief. So he wasn't quite as bad as she thought he was. He supposed one divorce was a better track record than two, but did it really matter?

"Her name was Alysson," he said. "She had no sense of humor, and we divorced ten years ago. Since then I haven't been too anxious to dive into another marriage. Last I heard, she'd moved out to Southern California, remarried and had a couple of kids. We don't communicate. I wish her well."

"But there are no others?"

"Other women. I'm not a monk. But not other ex-wives . . . and no other women currently. You've never been married?"

"No."

"You don't make mistakes."

"Sometimes I think I try too hard not to. Why didn't you correct me when I suggested you had more than one ex-wife?"

He gestured to their waiter for coffee and said matter-of-factly, "At the time I was doing a job. You were supposed to do the talking and the assuming, and I was supposed to do the listening—"

"And the judging."

"That's right."

For the first time he observed a hint of uncertainty and even guilt in her deep turquoise eyes. "I was just repeating a rumor I'd heard. Sometimes I should keep my mouth shut, I know, but at the time you were either a prospective client or a snake-in-the-grass columnist out to get me. I— Were you embarrassed?"

"Miffed would be more like it. As you should have gathered by now, I don't embarrass easily."

The waiter came with coffee, and Page smiled. "Or give up easily."

"Sweetheart, I don't give up at all."

"I don't know why—I don't even know if I *want* to know why—but I find that encouraging."

He grinned. "Good."

She insisted they split the bill down the middle and paid her half with two crisp tens. Chris's twenty looked rumpled next to them. "What do you do," he said, "iron your money?"

"Cash machines."

"Oh, right. I've never bothered getting a cash card. Too much like having access to free money."

"I can't tell you how many clients I've had to recommend turn in their bank cards. It's very easy not to write down withdrawals and even easier to get cash instead of learning to manage cash. But handled properly, they can be a tremendous convenience and timesaver. It all depends on the personality of the user." She grinned suddenly. "Am I lecturing again?"

"Yes."

"But I'm not making judgments," she said, serious. "What matters isn't whether or not you can manage a cash card. It's *knowing* that you can or can't, knowing yourself. I admire clients who come to know themselves."

"Even if what they know about themselves and have accepted would drive you out of your mind to have to live with?"

She looked him straight in the eye; he liked that kind of directness, even when, as now, it made him uncomfortable. "I don't have to live with it."

"At night you can go home to your nice clean, organized, color-coded condominium."

"Exactly."

"Not much potential for romance with clients, then, is there?"

"None whatsoever."

"Good. I'm glad I never hired you."

"But you still—" She cut herself off, then stood and pulled on her coat.

"I still what? I still have a disorganized life-style? I'm still *unsuitable*?"

He was half teasing, half serious, but she didn't answer, just walked past him. But he caught up with her quickly. "I'm still unsuitable," he persisted, "and you're still attracted to me. That's it, isn't it?"

"*Yes!*" She shoved her hands into her coat pocket and whirled around to face him. "Yes, it is. And doesn't the idea of being attracted to *me* scare the hell out of *you*?"

"Uh-huh," he said, and then smiled as a cool breeze made them both shiver. It was easy to forget that on spring nights the temperature could fall fast. "But I like to live dangerously."

ALL HER RULES of common sense told Page to say goodnight to Chris in the plush lobby of the Four Seasons Hotel. At most, to have a drink with him in the lounge. She did neither. Her rules suddenly seemed to her too rigid, too confining: she had to be more flexible.

Nonsense, she told herself, *you've got a tenacious case of spring fever, and you just don't want tonight to end.*

But she spun around in front of him and asked, "Would you like to come up?"

He said sure. Later she might need to try to blame something else—the clear night sky, the starlight—for her actions. But now she knew she was the one responsible for what she was doing, what she was feeling, not the stars or the weather. What mattered to her now was that being with Chris Battle felt right. She wanted to get inside his energy and spontaneity and flow with whatever it did to her. Dangerous, perhaps. But the desire was there, and it was as undeniable as the air they breathed. And it was her conscious choice to act on that desire.

They didn't speak again until they were inside her condominium and had kicked off their wet, muddy shoes. Spring in New England was seldom the driest of seasons. Page liked the look of Chris padding across the thick carpet of her living room in his stocking feet. He seemed so strong and capable. As if, in some intangible, imprecise way, he belonged there.

She asked if he wanted a glass of brandy.

"If you're having one, sure."

"At the rate I'm going," she said, laughing, "I may have two or three."

"You're living dangerously, too, huh?"

"Mmm."

The brandy was in the dining room. She poured two glasses and was surprised at how steady her hands were, and it occurred to her that, indeed, she wasn't the least bit nervous. Just crazy, she thought, returning to the living room. She found Chris standing at the big windows looking out across the Public Garden at glittering Beacon Hill. A plane was flying low over the city on its way into Logan Airport. Chris hadn't heard her come in. Page took the opportunity to study his slouching yet alert figure, hands stuffed in pants pockets, the back of his cotton shirt wrinkled, its sleeves rolled up above his wrists. Chris Battle at ease. Was he ever not at ease? It intrigued her that he could be so comfortable around her, but she was glad that he was. She hadn't taken any great pains to be frivolous and flirtatious. No pains at all, in fact. If anything, from the very beginning she'd been an even starchier version of herself. But he didn't seem deterred.

He was, after all, the most relentless man she'd ever met.

"Here you go," she said.

He turned and smiled, taking the glass from her. "I left a light on in my apartment."

"You do that a lot."

His eyebrows went up, but there was pleasure in his eyes. "You've been spying on me?"

"Well, I . . . yeah, I guess so."

"Shameless."

It was his toast. They clinked glasses and sat on the rug with their backs against the couch. Page stretched out her legs and noticed she had a tiny run in her stockings from her little toe up to her ankle bone. Chris noticed, too. He slid his big toe from one end of the run to the other. Heat radiated up her calves and thighs and spread throughout her, and it was all she could do to hang on to her brandy.

"Ruined," he said. "Do you have a use for wrecked nylon stockings?"

"I save them for my niece—my brother's daughter—and she makes dolls' faces out of them."

"Waste not, want not."

"She asked me to."

"Page, I'm not making fun of you," he said gently. "I admire your frugality, that you can live in an incredible apartment like this and still feel the need to save nylon stockings. Me, it doesn't matter a whole hell of a lot where I live, and when something's had it, I toss it. Of course, when *I* think something's had it and someone else thinks so may be two entirely different things. I know a number of people who believe most of my working wardrobe ought to be tossed." He shot her a look. "Do *not* analyze or lecture me on what I just said."

"I wasn't going to," she told him, sipping her brandy.

He laughed, incredulous. "Liar. You know, you keep up and I'm going to have to start counting your lies. Do organized people lie more than disorganized people?"

She laughed back at him. "Given your own track record, I'd say not. Want me to count up all your lies? We'd be here all night!"

"Sounds good to me. Let's start—"

He was cut off by the ringing of the telephone. Page extricated her foot from under his and went into the kitchen to answer it. Her knees felt wobbly, but it had nothing to do with nervousness. It had to do with still feeling the warmth of Chris's body next to hers and her having stuffed her foot into her mouth, run stocking and all. *We'd be here all night. . . .* What was the matter with her?

"Hey, there," Millie said. "William and I are downstairs in the lobby. Can we come up?"

"Well . . ."

"If not, it's okay."

"No, it's fine. By all means."

"On our way."

When she rejoined Chris in the living room, she sat on the edge of a chair and said, "That was Millie. She and William are downstairs."

"You told them to stay down there, didn't you?"

He spoke in a near growl that made Page realize he very definitely had other plans, that he *wanted* them to be alone together. She shuddered with a fresh wave of desire and wondered if her body was getting out of control. But she said primly, "No, I did not. Why should I?"

"You're being thickheaded on purpose. But if you want me to spell it out, I will. Don't think I'm afraid, Page B."

"You? Hardly. I wouldn't think fear is one of your major vices."

"Are you implying I have major and minor vices? How come you have only two and I have a whole damn list?"

She barely controlled a smile and maintained a look of pure smugness. "Genetics, I would think."

"Page B., the only reason I'm not going to tackle you for that comment is that we have friends on their way up. But I promise you, I will have my revenge. What's more, Ms Superiority, *we* are going to talk."

"Talk? We've been talking for hours!"

"About lobster eyeballs and run stockings—*not* about a certain note I left in an envelope for you and *not* about what happened before we went out to dinner."

She gave a nonchalant shrug. "What's there to say?"

"Lots." He rolled onto his knees in front of her, and for a second she thought he was going to plead with her. But Chris Battle wasn't the pleading type. He stood, and before she could think of a comeback, he took her chin in one hand and kissed her hard. "But go ahead and bring on William and your friend Millie. I'm not going anywhere."

She grinned at him, feeling a little dizzy from the kiss. "You are a determined man, Christopher Battle."

He sat on the couch. "Does that scare the hell out of you?"

"No, I find it quite encouraging."

William and Millie had six-year-old Beth with them. They'd all been over at Faneuil Hall Marketplace "grazing" on the dozens of food booths, people-watching and apparently not doing a very good job of telling Beth no. The little girl sauntered in boasting a new Red Sox cap, an oversize Boston sweatshirt and an armload of knickknacks, most of which, Millie complained, would end up under Beth's bed by tomorrow. All Page could think of was like mother, like daughter. Millie had never let her organizing friend touch her life . . . and Page wouldn't, even if Millie asked. Their friendship was too important.

Millie had brought a couple of dozen warm chocolate chip cookies with them, but when she saw Chris in the living room, she whispered to Page, "I didn't realize you had male company."

"It's Chris Battle."

"Aha. So you did do dinner, huh? We'll get lost."

"No, it's all right. Really."

Millie started to scowl, but Beth had already made her way to the refrigerator and was pulling out a carton of milk, and William had spotted Chris and was saying hello. "Well, I guess I don't have much choice." She gave Page a bawdy wink, adding, "Anyway, cookies will give you a boost of energy you'll need to burn off."

"*Millie!*" Page warned, but her friend ignored her and followed William into the living room.

Page made introductions as Beth settled on the floor with her glass of milk. She was tall for her age and outspoken like her mother. She was also Page's goddaughter. Whatever Beth had already consumed, it wasn't enough to make her wince at the prospect of chocolate chip cookies, but Page and Chris had skipped dessert, and Millie and William were always ready for a splurge. They sat around discussing the Red Sox prospects, and in short order a dozen cookies disappeared.

After that William Norton and the Friedenbachs did.

"Battle's a lot nicer in person than he writes," Millie whispered on her way out.

"He's on his best behavior tonight."

"Not for long, I'll wager."

The door shut before Page could choke her.

"Don't those two make an odd pair?" she reflected when she returned to the living room, where Chris was back on the floor in front of the couch.

"Whatever works."

"I guess. I worry about Millie, though. She's tough and it's no easy trick to pull the wool over her eyes, but she's impulsive. Last year she got so sick of winter she packed her bags one Thursday morning, picked up Beth from school and drove straight to the airport. They got on a plane flying standby. She didn't care where it was going as long as the destination was above sixty degrees."

Chris was holding back a laugh. "Where'd they end up?"

"Jamaica. They stayed until Monday and flew back in time for Beth to be back at school on Tuesday morning. William isn't that . . . spontaneous, is he?"

"Well . . ."

"Tell the truth."

"You're the one who organized him. You must know."

"Some things people refuse to tell their organizers," she said lightly. "You know, like analysts."

"Page—"

"I'm serious. If I'd been acting professionally instead of just being her friend, Millie never would have told me about that trip to Jamaica. As it was, she called and asked me if I wanted to come along."

"Did you?"

"Want to? Yes, very much. You remember last winter. It was awful. But I didn't go. I couldn't. I had commitments. And what kind of example would that have set for my clients? Anyway, that doesn't answer my question about William. Would he ever do anything like that?"

"I don't know, but I wish he would. He's gotten to be a workaholic—almost a recluse—since his divorce. He lives for his work and doesn't really go out much."

"Unless you're bribing him with hockey and basketball tickets."

Chris gave her an unrepentant look as she sat with her legs folded and her spine straight about a yard from his feet. "Why do you think I chose sports tickets instead of money? He needs to get out more. He used to be pretty impulsive. No trips to Jamaica, but he liked to do unexpected things, like buy a dozen roses for his wife for no reason or go on spontaneous day trips to New Hampshire or Vermont. But his wife was the type who only saw the money that went into the roses and wished he'd bought her a blouse or a blender instead, and who preferred one big vacation a year and the rest of the time to stay home weekends and wash the car or mow the lawn. William drove her crazy. She couldn't appreciate him for who he is—and vice versa, I have to admit."

"Sounds as if they were just too different," Page said, hating the note of dread in her voice.

"Not different in the right ways. There are differences that are compatible, enriching, and there are those that aren't. Theirs weren't." Chris drew up his knees and looked over the tops of them. "But we're not supposed to be talking about Millie Friedenbach and William Norton, are we?"

Page shook her head and picked rug fuzz off her dress, aware its hem had ridden way up above her knees when she folded herself up in a tailor squat. "Heart-to-heart talks have to be spontaneous," she said, not looking at Chris. "You can't plan them."

"You're not comfortable talking about our relationship."

It was a statement, but she said, "That's right. And don't say 'Okay, then tell me about yourself,' because that seems contrived, too. I figure all that stuff will come out as we spend more time together."

Chris rolled onto his knees and, stretching out on his stomach, propped himself on his elbows at her side. He said quietly, "So you do want us to spend time together."

She faked a nonchalant shrug and said teasingly, "Do I have a choice?"

"Yes." He inched closer, all his concentration on her. "Yes, you do have a choice. Always."

"I was just—" She broke off with a sigh. "I was just not being very funny. I know I have a choice. If you were doing a column on me, maybe not. But you're not. And anyway, yes, I do want us to spend time together. I'd like to get to know you better."

He smiled, and she could see the relief in his eyes. "But long talks deep into the night aren't your thing."

"I'm not really a talker. . . ."

"You'd rather listen."

She laughed a little. "And organize."

Reaching out with one finger, he drew a circle on her exposed knee. "But of course."

Transfixed, she watched the motion of his finger and took a breath that was meant to be deep but wasn't. Its shallowness, the movement of his finger, made her winded and slightly dizzy. For a moment she stopped breathing and just listened. All she could hear was Chris's steady breathing. It was strangely comforting.

"Tell me," she said, "that night you called with your 'two questions' . . . were you really taking me up on my offer?"

"What do you think?"

"No. But did you have two questions? Ever since I cut you off I've been wondering."

He began to make wider circles, using two fingers and moving higher, onto her thigh. "Yeah, I did."

"Were they legitimate?"

"To me they were."

"That leaves a lot of leeway."

"Now, now," he chided, not offended.

"What were they?"

"You really want to know?" He scooted another few inches closer and drew a circle whose circumference licked the edge of her hem high on her thigh. "All right. But do you still plan to answer them 'honestly and to the best of your ability'?"

His fingers were making her shiver, not with cold but with the spidery sensations they sent radiating through her. She took a moment to answer and finally said, "Sure, why not?"

"Okay. First question. What's the *B* in Page B. Harrington stand for?"

She grimaced. "And the second?"

"You have to answer the first one first."

"It's not a legitimate question, and you know it."

"Bertha?"

"No."

"Beatrice."

"No, now—"

"Belinda."

"*No.* Look, I'll tell you if you tell me what the *O* in Christopher O. Battle stands for."

"Another deal."

"And you don't make deals, so let's forget middle names. What's the second question?"

He suspended his circle making and gave her a direct, unwavering look. "Do you want us to make love?"

"*That's* the kind of question you ask in interviews?"

"Ass. It's the kind of question I ask beautiful, organized, turquoise-eyed women who make me crazy with ultimatums and their uncanny ability to upstage me. It's the kind of question I ask *you*."

She leaned back on her elbows and said lightly, "I figured that."

He gazed at the full length of her, his eyes lingering on her stomach, then her breasts, then her eyes. His hand was still on her knee. She could see herself taking quick, shallow breaths. She could feel her breasts swelling and see her nipples hardening beneath her dress. Since Chris Battle missed nothing, she didn't think he'd missed those very obvious indications of what the answer to his question would be.

He asked, "Are you going to answer honestly and to the best of your ability?"

There was something in his expression she hadn't seen before, and at first she didn't recognize it for what it was: uncertainty. It couldn't be something he liked to feel, or even liked to tolerate. He didn't measure the control over his life in terms of schedules and systems and organized working conditions but in terms of spontaneity and emotional certainty. She saw now that Chris Battle, tough and cynical as he was, could be hurt. That he could want. That he could feel rejection and anguish.

Simply put, he couldn't put words into her mouth. But he wanted to. He cared very much what her answer would be, but he wasn't sure what she was going to say.

"To answer to the best of my ability would probably mean not answering at all," she told him, hoping her sincerity would take any sting from her words. "I'm not very good at talking about my feelings. Traditionally women are supposed to be good at that sort of thing, but . . . I'm not." She looked away, grateful he hadn't tried to say anything. "But to answer honestly . . ." Swallowing, she bit her lip and wished all this came more easily to her. But she'd never been forthcoming about her feelings; she'd long avoided exposing herself in that way. Chris made a move toward her, and she knew instinctively that he wanted to tell her she didn't have to answer. But she refused to look at him, to signal an opening to interrupt, and finally she simply whispered, "Yes."

8

CHRIS SAT ON THE EDGE of Page's neatly made bed and watched her pull the drapes, the lights of Beacon Hill—including the one in his attic window—disappearing. Her bedroom was sophisticated and feminine, done in pale neutrals, spotless. No dust under the bed; he'd already peeked. And he hadn't said a word when he saw that her drawers weren't labeled after all.

He could tell she was feeling a little self-conscious. But she smiled when she turned back to him.

"You're sure about this?" he asked, although he could see no indication in her face that she wanted to change her mind and ask him to leave.

"Yes. I know what I'm doing."

"I've no doubt that you do."

He sensed what her admission had cost her: a bit of that control she prized so highly. In admitting she wanted to make love to him, she'd made herself vulnerable.

"But I think I know something of how you feel," he went on softly. "For us to move forward, there are going to be risks—for both of us."

There was a touch of surprise in her expression as she looked at him. "Thank you for understanding that. But I don't have a high degree of risk tolerance." She pulled open a drawer on her bedside stand and tossed him a little package. "See what I mean? I leave as little as possible to chance."

Chris blew dust off it and grinned when he saw what it was. He ignored her slight blush. "Always prepared, huh?"

She laughed. "I also keep bottled water, powdered milk and canned goods, too."

He arched a brow, not sure he wanted her to know just yet how much the dusty package inflamed him. "What more does one need?"

"Are you offended?" she asked, sitting down beside him.

"Are you kidding? I'm sitting here on your bed and you hand me the means of keeping us from getting into a mess and you think I might be offended? Sweetheart, what I am is turned on." He grabbed her around the waist and pulled her down flat on the bed, sideways under him. She was so damn lean and sexy. He grinned at her. "It must be the dust."

As he held himself above her, he lowered just his mouth to hers, forcing himself not to pounce. Her lips were dry and tasted faintly of brandy. He moistened them with his tongue. Desire rushed through him, urging him toward her, but still he held back. Her lips parted, and his tongue delved in. He moaned at the sweet taste of her, every fiber of his body tensed with wanting her.

She reached up and grabbed his sides. He could feel the indentation of each of her fingers as they dug into the solid muscle just under his ribs. Her tongue circled his with such heat and urgency he could barely hold himself under control. He wanted to take her now, just tear off her clothes and his and get on with it.

But he eased back and smiled, feeling his stiffness as he held his ache for her so rigidly in check. She was breathing as hard as he was, her face flushed with longing, further inflaming him.

"You haven't changed your mind?" he asked wryly.

"No!"

It came out as an emphatic breath.

"Good," he murmured, slowly sliding his hand up her thigh, "because I've never wanted anyone as much as I do you right now."

His hand stopped at the top of her panty hose, and he helped her out of them and her underpants, shuddering at the feel of her soft, warm skin under his hands.

He cupped her bottom and kissed her again. "I can't stand this...."

"Then don't," she whispered hoarsely, tearing at his clothes.

They pulled them off together and tossed them on the floor. "Want me to tidy up?" he asked.

"Not funny, Battle."

She was breathless as she lay back on her elbows, her dress hiked up, and let her gaze travel from his eyes down to his toes. There was a look of eagerness and longing in her expression that overwhelmed him with passion and a keen sense of rightness.

"Page B.," he said, his voice hoarse with the frustration of wanting her, "I wish you knew how many times I've looked out across the Public Garden and wondered if there was a woman out there who'd make me feel the way you do.... I wish *I* knew. You can see how much I want you—"

He broke off, moving toward her, and she surprised and further aroused him by giving him a secretive little grin. "I guess it was the dust," she said. "I'll have to remember that."

With a lust-filled growl he pushed her gently back on the bed, following her down as he scooped her up in his arms. He never wanted to let her go. He felt himself swelling not only with desire, but with a kind of emotion he'd given up on ever having the chance to feel. It nearly took his breath away. His entire being was filled with the feel of her, the soft smell of her, the possibilities of her. He couldn't imagine himself without her.

"Chris . . . I want you. I *need* you."

All he could manage was to speak her name, but he could hear all his tortured longing in his whisper.

She slipped her arms around his back and pulled him on top of her, and this time it was she who found his mouth. Her tongue plunged in, and her dress was hiked up above her hips . . . and all he knew was a passion so great he lost all sense of time and place. There was only her.

She was arching toward him, rubbing erotically against him, her every move telling him that they had gone beyond words. He started to get rid of the dress, but she shook her head never mind and grabbed at him. It was all he could do to deal with the matter of protection; he tore the package with his teeth and it was done.

He didn't know if he'd cried out or she had or they both had. He only knew that he was suddenly surrounded by the liquid warmth of her and his world had exploded. There was no longer a need to hold back. He couldn't.

And she urged him on, grabbing his hips and urging him into her. He thrust deep and hard, and she responded with a wild abandon that made his heart pound. And she pulled him deeper and harder until his head was spinning and his body burning and his world a mass of volcanic fire. Her fingers dug into his buttocks and she cried out, not holding back, either. Then they both were thrashing together, their release coming simultaneously, in great, monstrous bursts of flame that left them gasping and spent . . . and utterly satisfied. For him, never so satisfied. Never so at peace with himself and his future.

This is where I belong, he thought, holding her. *Now . . . forever.*

PAGE WOKE UP shaking violently, her pulse racing. She didn't know where she was. Somewhere she wasn't sure she belonged. Somewhere she didn't understand.

She couldn't remember ever being so terrified.

She bolted upright in her bed and gulped in a breath, then forced herself to let it out slowly as she tried to calm herself. Had she had a nightmare? What was wrong?

Suddenly she realized she was naked. The air was chilly, and goose bumps had broken out on her arms. Shivering, she pulled the covers up over her shoulders and looked around the room. It was her bedroom. Everything there was familiar. What she'd picked out, bought herself. What she knew. Waking up, she'd felt herself in alien territory. But nothing had changed.

She glanced at the figure with the tousled dark hair sleeping alongside her.

Everything had changed.

It was after dawn. A shaft of sunlight angled through a crack in the drapes and hit the pale rug. She felt uncomfortable having no sense of what time it was; usually she could guess within thirty minutes. What was it now? Five in the morning? Six?

She glanced at her clock radio and felt a stab of panic: 8:30.

Eight-thirty!

She threw back the covers and leaped out of bed but stopped herself so abruptly she stumbled. It was Saturday.

She'd forgotten.

She'd never forgotten what day it was.

Feeling foolish, she sat back on the edge of the bed, but it was too cold, and she had to decide whether to get up and put on her robe or climb back under the covers.

She got up and put on her robe.

The woman who looked back at her in the bathroom mirror seemed somehow different. There was a rosiness to her skin and a glow in her eyes that she'd never noticed before. It wasn't just because she'd made love last night; she knew better than that. It was because she'd made love with Chris Battle. After that first time she'd gotten out of her dress, and they'd turned out the lights and made love once more, slowly, taking the time to explore each other's bodies. She remembered his whispers about how she felt to him and what her caresses did to him. His talk had made her want him even more. But she'd said so very little. He'd seemed to understand and hadn't asked for more than she could give.

Her pulse quieted and she no longer shook. Whatever had caused it, her terror had subsided. Nevertheless, she felt ill at ease. She didn't like waking up in her own bed feeling so damn scared—

No, that isn't it!

She hadn't been scared. Not at all. What she'd felt was the panic of being out of control.

"Morning."

She turned and managed to smile at Chris, standing unabashedly—and magnificently—naked in her bathroom doorway. "Hello."

"Up early, aren't you?"

"I rarely sleep past eight, even on weekends."

"Even when you've been up half the night?"

"Apparently so. Coffee?"

He nodded, his gaze searching hers. But she averted her eyes and, dashing past him, told him he looked like a werewolf with his two-day growth of beard. He growled behind her, and she laughed, her uneasiness seeming so silly now with him awake. She scrambled out of the bedroom, making it to the kitchen without being attacked. In a few minutes he joined her, showered and with a towel wrapped around him but still, of course, unshaved.

"You look downright roguish," she told him, then added silently, *and sexy as hell.*

"Good. I feel pretty damn roguish, let me tell you. I can't remember the last time I was awake at 8:30 on a Saturday morning. You do this *every* week?"

"No, never. I'm always up much earlier. My cleaning woman comes at nine—"

"*What?*"

"Relax. She has four sons."

It wasn't good enough for Chris, and he tramped back into the bedroom and got dressed, grumbling loud enough for Page to hear him from the kitchen.

"Well, how was I supposed to know you were going to be here?" she yelled to him as she fixed coffee. "If we'd *planned* last night, I could have called her—"

"Dammit, woman, there are some things in life you just can't plan!"

She sighed, not the least perturbed by his outburst. "Are you really upset or just half pretending to be upset? You know, with you cynical types it's not always easy to tell. You're grouching about stuff so much of the time."

He groaned. "Now I'm supposed to be organized about how I get mad!"

"Just clear," she said, curiously calm.

"Why the hell is it I don't intimidate you?"

He'd made his way back to the kitchen just as the coffee finished dripping and the doorbell rang. Page shrugged as she headed past him to the entry. "In my profession," she said in a mock-cool tone, "one cannot be daunted by a disorderly mind."

If it hadn't been for Mrs. Rosanna's arrival, Page felt sure Chris never would have let that one pass. As it was, when they all had coffee together in the kitchen, he glowered at her in such a thrilling way she was reminded of the passion they'd shared during the night. Without any warning her pulse quickened and her hands began to tremble so badly that she had to put down her mug—and it had nothing to do with panic or terror. What was happening to her that she could be aroused by nothing more complicated than a look from him?

She felt . . . out of control.

Chris and Mrs. Rosanna were discussing the upcoming opening day at Fenway Park and the Red Sox chances for a pennant, but he seemed to sense Page's sudden discomfort and shot her a worried look. She smiled unconvincingly—at least Chris didn't look convinced. He pushed back his chair and rose. Already feeling out of breath, Page found herself taking in every inch of his hard male body, remembering the feel of the tanned skin under her fingers and hands . . . and tongue. She shivered with longing.

"Guess I'd better get back. Thanks for the coffee, Page. Mrs. Rosanna, I'll be watching for you at Fenway."

And he was gone. Page couldn't even bring herself to see him to the door.

SOMETHING WAS WRONG with Page B.

As Chris walked along the meandering paths of the Public Garden, enjoying the smells of early spring and the quiet of an early Saturday morning, he suspected he knew what had gotten under Page's lovely skin.

One Christopher O. Battle.

He wouldn't fit into her scheme of things. He didn't get up early on weekend mornings. He didn't shave regularly. He didn't have a cleaning woman. He didn't *clean*. He didn't plan when he was going to make love. He *had* come prepared for last night but hadn't wanted to embarrass her or otherwise prolong the business by flipping open his wallet and showing her what was tucked inside. He wasn't lazy and he wasn't irresponsible. He just wasn't . . . well, tidy.

But he also wasn't paranoid. He damn well knew that Page B. had had one hell of a time the night before. Even now at the blasted crack of dawn he could vividly remember how her body had shuddered with ecstasy under his, *with* his.

He'd fitted into her scheme of things last night, all right!

He understood that she was a little unnerved. So was he. He wasn't at all sure how Page B. Harrington would fit into *his* life. But she would fit there. Somehow he'd make room; he'd make the right adjustments. He'd shave every morning and get up at eight on Saturdays if she wanted him to.

Yet his pace had slowed, and he felt his shoulders sagging as he began to see the problem: he couldn't become someone else for her sake. It wasn't simply a question of his being unable to sacrifice his independence that way. It was also a question of who Page herself wanted him to be. As far as he could tell, it was him—with all his faults and quirks—that she had made love to last night.

Poor woman. She'd fallen for her unsuitable man.

PAGE HELPED Mrs. Rosanna give the condominium a thorough cleaning and afterward felt much better. There were no more cookie crumbs on the rug, and the milk glasses Millie, William and Beth had used were washed up and so were the two brandy glasses. They'd even given the coffee maker its monthly vinegar-and-water cleaning. Everything was shipshape and spotless.

And Page was bored.

Boredom often resulted from a lack of organization and priorities, but that wasn't her problem, at least not today. Mrs. Rosanna had left after lunch, and Page had the rest of the day to run errands, read her library books, write her letters home and play computer games. She had a nice neat list of Saturday priorities.

She wondered what Chris would say if he knew she sometimes played computer games. She wondered if—

It was useless. She couldn't stop thinking about him.

"I don't *want* to stop," she muttered, lunging for the telephone. She dialed his number and was relieved when he answered on the third ring. "Hi, it's me."

"Hello, me."

He sounded groggy—and delighted to hear her voice. A surge of energy made her tingle with excitement. "Were you sleeping?"

"Well . . . yes. You may be able to scrub floors after a night like we had, but we decrepit old journalists . . ."

"Decrepit, my foot. I probably should take a nap, but I can't. I'm too keyed up or something."

"Probably 'or something.'"

There was a sensual undertone to his words that didn't escape Page. "You do have a fine opinion of yourself, don't you? Well, I have an idea."

"Does it involve little colored circles that we have to stick on things?"

"No, it does not. Nor does it involve plastering poor innocent people who are just trying to make a living doing something Christopher O. Battle might not approve of. It involves maple sugaring."

"Maple what?"

"Sugaring. Actually, mostly maple syruping these days. I was thinking we could head out to western Massachusetts and check out a sugar shack, then spend the night at an inn and have blueberry pancakes with gobs of fresh syrup on them in the morning." She took a breath. "I'm being spontaneous."

"You certainly are. You mean *today*?"

"I guess. The sugar season doesn't last long. It might already be over, in fact. It depends if the trees have budded in the western part of the state yet. I'm sure it's still going on in northern Vermont, but that's a little far, I think. I— Do you think I'm crazy?"

"Yes. And I love it. I'll be right over."

"Well, I'll need a couple of hours to—"

"Page, spontaneous means *now*."

"No, it doesn't. It means resulting from a natural impulse, something not forced. I looked it up."

He was silent for a moment. Then he said, "So you don't feel any pressure from me to do this. You're being 'spontaneous' of your own accord."

"If it was of anyone else's," she said, "it wouldn't be spontaneous."

He laughed. "There's got to be a column in this somewhere. Okay, a couple of hours."

"No, no. Now's fine."

"You're sure?"

"Of course." She laughed and added in her best haughty organizer's tone, "The way I figure it, it'll be at least an hour before you get yourself pulled together enough to get over here."

"You think so?"

"Given the state of your apartment, I'd say so."

"That's a professional opinion?"

"Yes, but I won't charge you."

"What about you?"

She bit back a laugh. "If I need to, *I* can be ready in ten minutes."

CHRIS HAD TO HOOF IT, but he made it to Page's doorstep in ten minutes flat. He felt a surge of excitement when he knocked. Maple sugaring didn't intrigue him, but the prospect of spending the rest of the weekend with Page did. And it had been her idea. Spontaneous Page. He smiled and gave the door another tap with his knuckles.

"It is you," she said when she pulled open the door. "Will miracles never cease? Come on in."

He had a battered Lands End bag slung over one shoulder. He couldn't vouch for what was inside, but he was positive whatever it was would see him through the weekend. "Is that how you talk to clients?"

She tossed him a grin over her shoulder as she headed down the hall to her bedroom. "I wouldn't stay in business long if I did."

"Lucky I have a strong ego."

"Lucky we both do, sweets."

Wasn't she chipper this afternoon? Chris thought with amusement. "Does scrubbing floors always make you sarcastic?"

"It's the smell of clean tiles and waxed furniture that does it." From her tone he couldn't tell how serious she was. "Gives me quite a heady feeling. It's almost as good as sex."

That did it. He dropped his bag and was down the hall in a flash. She had her clothes for the weekend neatly folded on the edge of her bed and her back to him as she shook out a nightgown. A *nightgown*, he thought. What did she think she'd need that for?

He pounced.

Swinging one arm around her middle, he threw her off balance, and they fell onto the bed together. She groaned. "My clothes! Chris, dammit—"

"Compare *me* to a bottle of ammonia . . ."

"I wasn't. I was just kidding!"

"Too late."

He grabbed her sides and tickled her unmercifully, but Page B. Harrington wasn't one to acquiesce. She wasn't a scrawny bit of fluff, either. With great determination and no small amount of strength she went for *his* sides, and soon they were rolling all over her queen-size bed, laughing and tickling and making a general mess of her clothes, including those she had on. Her blouse had come untucked and was twisted . . . and it was just too tempting. Chris shoved one hand up it and felt her warm, smooth skin. His palm moved upward.

"*Don't* tickle there," she warned.

"I don't intend to."

He moved his hand over the soft swell of her breast and easily unhooked the front clasp of her bra. She murmured as his mouth covered hers. Under his palm he felt her nipple harden, and he rubbed it gently with his thumb as his tongue probed the inside of her mouth with the same rhythm. He felt himself hardening.

"I think we're going to get a late start," he said, coming up for air.

She grinned at him. "You're wrecking my spontaneity."

"I'd say this is 'resulting from a natural impulse,' wouldn't you?"

"Very natural . . . Chris!"

It wasn't a cry of anguish or warning, but of sheer delight—and he knew it. He'd trailed his hand down her side and slipped it inside her pants and down her bottom. He could feel her warmth and how much she wanted him. In seconds their clothes joined those she'd so neatly arranged, and he lay back on a heap of them and she climbed on top of him, straddling him and drawing him into her at once. She set the pace for their lovemaking, and it was a wild one. He held back and focused on her and her pleasure, watching her bite down on her lower lip and thrust herself down onto him, again and again. Only when he could hardly see from want did he stop watching her and shut his eyes as wave after wave of fulfillment washed over him.

Afterward he helped her refold her clothes and noticed that she'd lapsed into silence. "Are you okay?" he asked gently.

She nodded, putting things into her overnight bag in an organized manner that seemed so automatic to her. Unless he just shoved things into a bag, he had to concentrate on what went where so this wouldn't get wrinkled and that wouldn't get dirty and that wouldn't spill onto that. But she tackled packing with the same speed he did, just more efficiently. It was a trick, he decided, he'd have to learn. But he'd tell her that later.

"Page, do I scare you?"

"No!" She seemed startled by his question. "No, I guess I scare myself. But it's nothing to worry about. Shall we take my car?"

"Allow me, won't you? Believe me, I have the perfect vehicle for maple sugaring."

IT WAS A BIG GMC TRUCK of indeterminable vintage— and color. Something between gold and brown, Page decided. It was the sort of color only available for beat-up old trucks. It was parked on the street, and she had to laugh when she saw the prestigious Beacon Hill resident sticker.

"And you a famous columnist," she said. "I was expecting a Mercedes."

"The hell you were."

"All right, all right. I was expecting . . ." Sighing, she eyed the truck once more. "I guess I was expecting this."

"It gets me where I'm going. It's never been stolen or stripped and isn't likely to be. Other vehicles give way to it in a traffic jam—and you know how rotten Boston drivers are under the best of circumstances, so that's saying something, indeed."

"But what about your image? What if you need to impress someone?"

"First, I don't give a damn about my 'image.' Second, I've never needed to impress anyone...or wanted to. Third, if I did, this baby's impressive as hell. How many trucks do you know that have been on the road for twenty years?"

"Mercifully, none."

She was glad he realized she was only half serious and laughed as he unlocked the passenger door. "Correction," he said. "Now you know one."

He pulled the door open, and with a mock-chivalrous bow, helped her up onto the seat. With less ceremony he tossed the two bags onto the somewhat dubious-looking floor at her feet. The dashboard was dusty and the upholstery frayed, but when Chris climbed into the driver's seat beside her, he informed her that the engine ran like a top—at least for a twenty-year old truck. On the third try it started with a roar.

Chris grinned at her. "Love that sound. What do you drive?"

"A Pontiac sedan."

"There you go. Keep America working."

She didn't point out that the America he'd kept working was probably near retirement age. Nor when they began coughing down Beacon Hill did she point out that the gas gauge read empty. She herself *never* parked her car on an empty tank. But she kept quiet and relaxed as they bumped along to Route 2 West... without stopping for gas.

Finally she couldn't stand it anymore. "Um, do you plan to stop for gas on Route 2?"

He looked over at her. "I was wondering how long you'd sit on it. You notice everything, don't you?"

"Well, no, I don't think so. I just don't want to run out of gas."

"Trust me."

"I do. How far can you get when the gauge reads empty?"

"Miles and miles."

"That's rather vague."

"I know." He reached over and patted her knee. "Relax, darlin'. The damn gauge doesn't work."

9

ABOUT TWO HOURS LATER Page gave Chris directions to a farm just north of monstrous Quabbin Reservoir, a Depression-era public works project that had drowned five towns to provide water for metropolitan Boston. As the truck clattered up the road, Page said, "It's hard to imagine now what this area would be like if those five towns had continued to exist. Quabbin's become quite a wildlife preserve—bald eagles have returned. But it must have been difficult for people to give up their homes, move their dead . . . I don't think anyone'd get away with a project like that these days."

Chris gave her a suspicious look. "How do you know all this?"

"Oh. I grew up around here."

"I see."

She was quite sure he didn't, simply because she'd neglected to tell him a few salient facts—such as the sugar shack they were headed to was on Harrington property. But she didn't think he needed to know that just yet. She asked, instead, "Where did you grow up?"

"Suburban Boston."

"That covers dozens of towns. Did you move around a lot?"

"No. We always lived in the same house."

There was something about his tone that made her turn, but his expression was unreadable, and she couldn't tell what had caught her attention. "Does your family still live there?"

"Mmm."

"In what town?"

"Concord."

Concord was an expensive suburb west of Boston known for its beautiful colonial homes. She enjoyed shopping in Concord and strolling along its picturesque streets, where she didn't recall ever having seen a beat-up old truck parked. But perhaps Chris was from one of Concord's slightly less prestigious neighborhoods. She couldn't, however, think of a polite way to ask.

"Concord. Really? It's a beautiful town. No wonder you weren't worried about sending your mother a birthday card on time. You can just visit."

"Not in March," he said. "She and my father stay in Florida most of the winter. They have a place on Amelia Island."

"Oh."

She spoke absently, thinking fast about changing their route, but she knew it was too late. The familiar hill was coming up fast. She told Chris to take the next left, a back road that wound into the hills. They passed a small white clapboard house: Mr. Sadowski was out putting up his mailbox, which had obviously been knocked down by a snowplow. It happened every year. Page waved and noticed his look of surprise as the truck clattered through a series of potholes. The last time he'd seen her, she'd been in her dark blue sedan. Beat-up trucks hadn't been her style in years.

"Do you always wave at old men?" Chris asked.

"That's Mr. Sadowski."

"Uh-huh."

He obviously didn't understand, but why should he? Page coughed and added, "He was my closest neighbor growing up."

"Page..."

"Take the next right."

"The driveway with the dog sleeping in the middle of it?"

She nodded. "That's Gladiola."

Since there was no other traffic on the narrow road, Chris didn't bother to signal. He just glanced at Page as he made the turn. "Gladiola," he repeated.

She smiled at him and, her heart pounding, said, "My family's dog."

THE DRIVEWAY WAS UNPAVED, and for an anxious moment Chris thought they were going to get stuck in the mud. The truck, however, pulled through. Page gave him directions to a giant shallow puddle that served as a parking area in front of a shed painted barn red. About twenty yards to their left was the side entrance to a gray clapboard house that needed painting; none of its black shutters seemed to hang quite straight. The place was tucked on a hillside in the generally colder west-central part of the state, where spring didn't come as early. There were still patches of snow in the woods behind the house and on the other side of the road; everywhere else it was muddy. A few chickens were scratching in the wet, pounded-down grass. Buckets and plastic milk jugs hung from every maple tree in the vicinity, catching the clear, sticky sap.

"I thought we came from the same kind of background," Page said sheepishly and, before he could respond, climbed down from the truck.

Gladiola, who looked to be half Labrador and part everything else, trotted happily up to meet her, and Chris watched in amazement as Ms Neatnik herself patted the grubby dog on its head. He was quite honestly taken aback. *This* was her home? But then he thought of the huge house in Concord where multiple generations of Battles had been raised—no, *bred*—and he supposed it would give her a similar shock.

An old man in a baseball cap and work clothes trudged out of the shed to see what all the commotion was about. Chris climbed out of the truck, and Page made introductions. "Grandpa, I'd like you to meet a friend of mine, Chris Battle." She turned to Chris and bit down on one corner of her mouth. "Chris, my grandfather, Will Tucker."

They shook hands, the old man's callused and half-frozen, but he didn't seem uncomfortable. He said, "That's a good-looking truck you have there."

Instant approval. Chris grinned at Page's scowl and then followed her inside, where it was bedlam. He was introduced to various sisters, brothers, cousins and in-laws and a half-dozen infants and preschoolers who were visiting. Page's mother was an attractive woman with gray-streaked auburn hair who didn't seem to let much bother her, including surprise guests. She invited them to make themselves at home; there was food in the refrigerator if they were hungry.

"It's like this every weekend," Page explained as she and Chris went back outside. "Mother never knows who's going to show up. She and my grandfather live here. They have about two hundred acres, most of it woodland—a Yankee farm. It's kind of the family homestead."

"What about your father?"

"He lives in Arizona. He left when I was in high school."

"Divorced?"

She shook her head. "They never bothered. He turns up three or four times a year for a visit, but he hates New England winters. He has a condo near Phoenix."

"What does he do?"

"Whatever he feels like doing. My family always manages to get by. They just don't make it easy. They thrive on living on the edge, I guess."

"But you don't. You're the planner."

She laughed. "Ms Organizer, to quote a famous columnist."

He was relieved to see that any awkwardness she might have felt when they first rolled into the driveway had vanished, and he thought he understood: for better or worse, this was her home.

Grandpa Tucker put them to work fixing the fence around what promised to be a monstrous vegetable garden and filling a dozen bird feeders with seeds and hauling sap and building an outdoor fire and digging out the big tub to boil down the first of the sap ... *and my God*, Chris thought, *he could work a horse to death!* Meanwhile, Grandpa fiddled with a small tractor. At various times adults and kids filed out of the house and played, pestered or helped. Chris began to understand where Page had gotten her capacity for work. He'd worked up a hell of a sweat himself.

"How long does this stuff have to boil before it starts looking like syrup?" he asked, dubiously eyeing the bubbling cauldron.

"Hours. It takes about forty gallons of sap to make one gallon of syrup."

"No wonder the damn stuff's so expensive. I feel like a witch, don't you?"

"Don't let Grandpa hear you say that. He's very practical about this sort of work. You'll make him think you're from the eastern part of the state."

"A city boy?"

"Uh-huh. I guess you should be glad you don't drive a Mercedes."

"But you'd have had me drive it here, anyway, if I did?"

"Why not?" She grinned at him as she stirred the sap, the heat of the fire flushing her cheeks.

"Grandpa Tucker wouldn't have approved."

"I know."

"So that's it. If your family approves, I'm doomed."

She laughed, keeping the tone of their conversation light, although Chris suspected he'd stumbled on a touchy subject. "A more precise definition of an unsuitable man than the one I gave you last night might be a man my family approves of. Silly, you think?"

"Damn silly."

Finally they let the fire die down and gathered with the rest of the family at the long kitchen table for chili, corn bread and salad. Chris did feel their approval. The young ones razzed him about whatever they could think of—including his "Boston accent," which he didn't have, as far as he was concerned. The older ones got him talking about his column but made it obvious they'd never read it. He appreciated their bluntness. They took him for exactly what he presented to them at that moment at the supper table.

When dinner was finished, people began to leave, perfectly delighted that Page and Chris had volunteered to do the dishes.

He said, "They're quite a crew. And you never forget a birthday?"

"Nope."

"Amazing."

"Once you have a system in place, it's not amazing at all."

"But the rest of your family isn't so organized."

"No. Not that they forget things. It's just that they're always on the brink of disaster. I can't live like that, and I've quit trying to pretend I can. I need a calendar, money in the bank, plans, goals, grocery lists. Maybe sometimes I'm too rigid, but I couldn't stand this level of . . . spontaneity."

Chris threw a towel onto one shoulder as he got the empty chili pot off the stove. "You seem to get along with your family."

"I hope so. I just don't try to change them, and they don't try to change me. It all works out, at least most of the time."

"About tonight . . . did you plan to stay over here?"

Page laughed, her eyes twinkling. "Are you kidding? Grandpa would have us out cutting wood next. No, as it so happens, there *is* an inn nearby."

"Did you make reservations?"

"Why, Chris Battle," she said, "this is Page B. Harrington you're dealing with. You and the rest of the

Tucker-Harrington family would have just winged it. Me, I called ahead."

They thanked Grandpa Tucker and Mrs. Harrington for a wonderful day and got out of there before the old man could notice his woodpile was getting low and give them just one more job to do before they left.

It was Chris who suggested they stop back there in the morning. "Your grandfather offered me a pint of syrup when it's done."

"Don't let him exploit you. He'll do anything to have someone to order around. You can buy maple syrup, you know."

"Yeah, but it's not the same as making my own."

"There's no hope. You like them, don't you?" She shook her head and sighed. "And they like you. I might add, Christopher O. Battle, that although I haven't brought home scores of men, you're the first who didn't either run at the sight of them or get chased off."

"Question is, is that a point in my favor or a point against me?"

She shrugged, leaving the question unanswered, as if she didn't take him seriously. Chris didn't push for an answer. But he *was* serious: if Page didn't fancy herself fitting in with her own family, would it matter that much that he did? The Harringtons weren't anything like the Battles of Concord—with whom Page would fit in beautifully—but he did like them.

And damned if he was going to let old Will Tucker reap all the rewards of his hard work today. As he drove along the highway to the inn, Chris could almost smell the pancakes and his very own maple syrup he was going to fix Page and him one morning for breakfast . . . one morning soon, he thought. Very soon. Her world had become his, and he wasn't going to back out of it just because they didn't have everything down to their handwriting in common.

HE HAD FIT RIGHT IN.

Page sighed as she headed up the wide stairs at the adult education center where she was teaching her Monday-night class on getting organized. She had been incredibly distracted all day. Her new clients ran a small, wonderful café in Cambridge's Porter Square, but they needed help—*lots* of help—in making the best use of their limited time and space. They'd fed her an apricot-filled croissant for midmorning snack and a monumental sandwich of lean corned beef on homemade rye bread for lunch, with, of course, as much hot coffee as she could drink. And there were the warm chocolate chip oatmeal cookies for dessert. She'd skipped dinner.

But food and work hadn't stopped her from thinking about her weekend with Chris. They'd stayed in a charming inn and had made love most of the night, sleeping late the next morning—after she'd awakened him at eight o'clock. He'd been groggy at first, but it hadn't lasted. They'd had a fabulous breakfast of buttermilk pancakes dotted with tiny wild blueberries and moistened with pure maple syrup, Vermont cob-smoked bacon, fresh fruit and several cups each of coffee.

Then Chris had suggested they head back over to her mother and grandfather's place and burn off all those extra calories. When they got there and trekked off into the woods with Grandpa, she began to wonder. Did Chris fit in *too* well? She'd lit one hell of a fire and boiled down the rest of the sap, finishing it off in the kitchen with her mother, who'd learned long ago not to ask her daughter questions about her love life. They'd talked business and animals and family.

During the entire trip back to Boston Chris had raved about what a great guy her grandfather was and how laid-back her mother was and what a beautiful place they had. He'd used words like *relaxed*, *uninhibited*, *easygoing*, *unperturbable*.

In her world, red-flag words.

He'd said, "Your mother and grandfather seem to take life as it comes."

That was her whole point, which he didn't seem to understand.

Because he fit right in.

She'd replied through clenched teeth, "See why I live in Boston?"

"Yes," he said, "I do. It's barely two hours away. You can go to your mother's just about whenever you want."

In other words, he hadn't seen at all.

They'd arrived back in Boston late, and he'd asked her if she'd be embarrassed to have him drop her off at the Four Seasons in his truck. She explained that if Mother and Grandpa could visit her in *their* truck, he could damn well drop her off in his. So he had. He'd smiled at her in lieu of a kiss and promised he'd be in touch soon.

When she'd returned to her condo at 4:15 that afternoon, there was a message on her machine from him. "Dinner tonight?" Nothing more. She'd called ten times before finally getting through to him minutes before she had to leave for class.

"I'm not available for dinner tonight," she'd said, and explained. "Sorry. Tomorrow night, maybe?"

He hadn't made her feel guilty for having to work, which she'd appreciated. But he'd asked, "Where's this class?"

"At the adult ed center on Commonwealth Avenue."

"Meet me after for a drink?"

"Okay. But I might have students with me."

"No problem. You can bring them up to my place."

"Your place?"

"Something wrong?" he asked, his voice low and very sexy. There was no doubt what he was intimating.

"Chris, I . . ." She'd paused. "I don't know how long I'll be able to stay."

"Don't worry. We'll just see what develops."

Now as she went into the classroom and smiled at the dozen students gathered at the single long table, she regretted not having been more direct. She *couldn't* just see what developed. She hadn't brought any clothes or cosmetics or even her facial cleanser, and she had to be up early tomorrow. Her clients had asked her to come by before the café opened at seven, which meant she had to leave her condo by six. No *way* could she spend the night with Chris and meet her business commitments.

But she wanted to. As she'd walked along Commonwealth Avenue, she'd thought of him . . . wanted him. Even when he wasn't with her, he filled her being with his presence. A few weeks ago she might have blamed spring fever. But now she knew it was more than that. Much more. She smiled. This madness wasn't going to go away with the beginning of summer!

She opened her leather portfolio and pulled out her notes as she greeted her students. Everyone seemed to have arrived on time. Not bad, she thought, pleased. She took a moment to compose herself before beginning.

The sound of footsteps echoed in the hall. Thinking it must be someone from another class, Page asked a student at the other end of the table to please close the door. As he rose, however, a deep, languid voice said, "Hold on a sec."

Chris Battle appeared in the doorway with his tousled dark hair and completely disarmed the rest of the class with his grin. The teacher, however, remained rigid.

"Sorry I'm late," he said, his gaze meeting hers briefly, and he sat down.

Page recovered her poise and managed to smile. She said to the class, "It seems in every course I teach there's *always* one incorrigible. Welcome, Mr.—"

"Battle," he supplied, deadpan. "Chris Battle."

The class made a collective gulp, and in a tight voice Page reassured them that "Mr. Battle" was there for personal reasons and wasn't—repeat, was *not*—there to do research on a column on professional organizers.

It amazed her when everyone groaned with disappointment. Chris's slate eyes flickered up to hers, as if to say, *See, I could've had your hide if I'd wanted to!*

She wondered if he'd get it yet, one way or the other. In a cool, professional voice she said, "Let's begin."

All the way down the table notebooks were opened and pens uncapped...except for Chris. He was the only student who hadn't brought anything to write on or write with. Without a word Page passed a sheet of paper and a sharpened pencil down to him and shot him a look that told him exactly what she expected. He complied. Uncrossing his legs and dropping his feet flat on the floor, he got to work.

10

As he ambled toward Page from his end of the table, Chris observed the way she tucked her leather case under one arm, with just enough tightly controlled anger that he knew she wasn't too pleased with him. Class was over. He hadn't done anything disruptive—except be there. Page had already gotten rid of any students who might have wanted to join her for a drink: presumably, he thought with a hint of foreboding, she wanted him all to herself.

"You could have told me you were going to be here tonight," she said. "Why didn't you?"

He shrugged, hoping to dissipate her anger by not letting it get to him. "I didn't have a chance. I didn't think of it until after I'd talked to you."

"It was a spur-of-the-moment decision?"

He didn't miss her scathing tone but replied evenly, "That's right."

She snorted in disgust and pounded out of the classroom and down the stairs, leaving him to follow if he so chose. He did. He admired her energy, but he thought her irritation with him a bit uncalled for. All he'd tried to do was show a little interest in her work. As he joined her on Commonwealth Avenue, he took a breath of the warm spring air. It was a romantic night.

"Page," he said, coming up beside her, "why are you so upset? It's not as if I acted like a jerk or anything. I didn't say a word."

"No, you just *sat* there."

"What was I supposed to do? Ask questions, take notes?"

"Not be there."

He tried humor. "I wanted to see Barracuda Harrington at work."

She spun around at him so hard and so fast he thought she was going to keep on spinning, like a top. But she had perfect control over herself and leveled those angry turquoise eyes at him. "There you go, that's it. *That's* my point. You were a distraction. I kept wondering what you'd think of my ideas. Every time I said a word, I thought about you and your column and how you could twist my words and make them sound dumb or stuffy or...or like I was running some kind of scam!"

"I made you self-conscious."

"Yes!"

"I'm sorry if I did. But I thought you understood that I have no intention of doing the column. My God, after this weekend how could I?"

She resumed walking down Commonwealth, still moving at a good clip. "But if you had still been working on your column, tonight would have been terrific research, right?"

"Yes." She'd never believe him if he tried to deny it. "Wish I'd thought of it while I was on the story. But that doesn't mean you said anything that was easy to make fun of. In fact, I was rather impressed. Look, I didn't go tonight because of my column or because I wanted to denigrate what you do. I went because I wanted to know more about what you do—about *you*, Page. I figured if you could read my column three times a week, I could show up at one of your classes."

They came to the corner of Commonwealth Avenue and Arlington Street. Straight ahead, across Arlington, was the Public Garden. Beacon Street ran parallel to Commonwealth on the left, Boylston Street on the right. If Page turned right, it meant she was calling it a night and heading home. If she turned left, it meant she was heading to his place.

She glanced at him, and he could see her anger had started to cool. "All I want is a little respect."

"Most of us do, but it's damn hard to get these days. Everyone's looking to dump on someone."

"Okay. All I want is *your* respect."

He smiled. "You've got it. Have I got yours?"

She sighed and smiled back. "Yes."

"But you and I both know that what we do isn't going to save the world. I try to give people a chuckle and maybe even something to think about over their morning coffee or on their subway ride to work. You try to help people make the best use of their available time, space and money. Our work gives us satisfaction and it's not dope dealing, but—"

"It's not brain surgery, either."

"Right."

"So I shouldn't take myself so seriously?"

He slipped his arm around her waist. "Let's just say I think you should cut yourself some slack once in a while."

She laughed. "And you, too?"

"Definitely!"

"Well," she said, patting his hand on her waist, "I have to admit it wasn't just because I thought you were going to poke fun at my work that made me feel self-conscious."

He loved the feel of her under his arm and wanted to get closer, much closer. "No?"

"Uh-uh. It was also because every time I looked over and saw those dark gray eyes of yours, I thought about this weekend and . . . well, it was very distracting."

"Good," he said, and dropped his arms so she would have complete freedom to pick which way she wanted to turn.

She turned left.

PAGE DIDN'T KNOW WHY she hadn't told Chris she didn't have time to visit and gone straight home. It was late. She was tired. She was still confused and, if not irritated, at least unsettled. Out of control. She wasn't sure what she'd do next—what he'd do. To cover for her uneasiness, she said she was hungry and pulled open Chris's refrigerator. It was not well stocked. She felt his gaze on her as she rummaged around for something to eat.

"Beer, hot dogs, o.j. What's in the jar? It looks like cornmeal."

"It is."

She glanced up at him, leaning against the stove as he watched her. "Stone-ground, huh?"

"Makes the best corn bread and hush puppies. Not Concord food, I know, but who cares? It suits me. As far as I'm concerned, no kitchen is complete without stone-ground cornmeal."

"Why's it in a jar?"

"There's some kind of weird leak inside the fridge. I didn't want the package to get wet."

"Why don't you get the leak fixed?"

"Not worth it. I'll just wait and buy a whole new fridge one of these days. It's been doing it for about five years, so I'm used to it."

Page sighed. *She* couldn't have tolerated a leaky refrigerator for more than a few days. She stuck her head back in the fridge and, pushing aside a jar of plain golden mustard, seized a carton of yogurt. "Great, just what I feel like."

But when she'd shut the refrigerator door, Chris was shaking his head. "I wouldn't if I were you."

"What's wrong?"

He pointed. "Check the date."

"*January* 9? But it's almost April!"

"I don't eat yogurt. Some friend left it here."

"And you just haven't gotten around to tossing it."

He grinned without apology. "Cleaning the refrigerator isn't high on my list of priorities."

"I should say." She deposited the offending carton in the trash. In her own routines she made it a weekly practice to give her refrigerator a clean sweep, when she brought her groceries in. Before the fresh stuff went in, the old stuff went out. Simple. But she doubted Chris Battle did much of anything to simplify his life; even weekly grocery shopping was beyond his capacity for organization.

"If you're hungry," he told her, "I can run over to Charles Street and fetch something."

"No, that's okay. I'll just have a beer."

"Allow me."

He got out two bottles, opening both and handed her one. "Wait, do you use a glass?"

She smiled. "This is fine."

The beer was very cold and very smooth—Chris spared no expense there—and Page felt herself begin to calm down. She hated feeling so jittery, and especially being unable to pinpoint exactly why. Perhaps it was just fatigue ... and the frustration of knowing she couldn't stay.

"Is something wrong?" Chris asked, his brow furrowing as he studied her. "Would you like to go sit down?"

She leaned against the refrigerator and sipped her beer. "I don't know. I'm just feeling a little jumpy."

He grinned, a wolfish, sexy grin that conjured up all that had passed between them over the weekend. She could almost *feel* his hand trailing up her inner thigh and felt a shiver as a thousand different sensations spread up her spine.

"Why's that?" he asked.

"Who knows?" She sighed, suddenly feeling silly. "My God, Chris, don't you feel like a couple of adolescents at a sock hop?"

"Hope if we were adolescents we wouldn't be drinking beer and thinking about what we're thinking about."

"True . . ."

But his smile vanished, and he said seriously, "Page, I'm making you uncomfortable. I want to know why."

If only I knew why! she thought, but suggested they go sit down. She waited until he'd sat on the couch before taking the chair catty-corner to him. Her instincts, such as they were, warned her that this wasn't the right time to snuggle up on the couch with him.

"Well?" he prodded.

She drank some beer. "I don't know why."

"You're good at sorting things out. Start sorting out what's making you sit on that chair over there instead of beside me on the couch."

Flopping back against the chair, she groaned. "Am I being that obvious? All right. If I sat beside you, I know we'd end up doing everything *but* talking—and we need to talk. I didn't know how much we needed to talk until I actually got up here, but now I guess I do. But I'm not sure I have my thoughts organized."

"Good," he said softly.

"What's that supposed to mean?"

"It means I want the unedited, unorganized, unadulterated truth. You can plug into all your communications skills and image-making skills and all that other stuff another time—with someone else. With me you can forget about control. You don't have to control me, and you don't have to control yourself. Just *be* yourself, Page. Spit out what you have to say, and we'll sort through it together."

"When you write a column, you have all your thoughts so neatly organized."

"That's right, I'm supposed to. It's my job. But you should see the garbage I have to write before I get everything written up so nice and tidily. The first draft of a thousand-word column can run ten or fifteen pages and be filled with contradictions, unsubstantiated accusations, incomplete thoughts, arguments that go nowhere, emotions that have no place in what I'm doing, inappropriate language—you name it. But I don't worry about it. Nobody's going to see it but me or someone I trust."

She licked her lips and sat up, resting her beer bottle on her knee and picking at the label. "What you're asking me to do, then, is to trust you."

He didn't hesitate. "Yes."

"And you think you've earned that trust?"

"Maybe not. But how do you know when someone has earned the right to be trusted? You won't know until you've gone ahead and trusted them and then been burned . . . or not burned. To trust is an act of faith."

She nodded, meeting his gaze. "A risk."

"What's the worst that could happen to you if you trust me?"

"You could betray that trust."

"How?"

"By not accepting what I feel and think as being valid, by not accepting me for who and what I am. The more honest and frank I am with you about my deepest fears and emotions, the more I'll have to lose if and when you leave."

"Aha. The more you invest in what we have here, the more you'll lose if it doesn't work out. Invest less, lose less. That's the risk, isn't it? With money you can make a calculated gamble. With romance—not so easy, is it? You can't have a falling-in-love plan the way you can have an investment plan. You've got to just roll with it. Maybe you can put your money in an account and know you're going to get eight-percent interest compounded whenever and however, but you can't know in advance a relationship is going to work out."

She looked at him with an expression that she was positive betrayed no indication she was going to back down. "Maybe not, but you can minimize your risk."

"In a word, humbug."

Obviously, she thought, she didn't intimidate him any more than he intimidated her: he felt awfully damn free to argue with her! "You can," she insisted. "Take me, for example. If I put my mind to it, I could only go out with men who fit, at least loosely, my idea of what the right kind of man for me is."

Chris scoffed. "How can you know the right kind of man if you haven't met him yet?"

"By looking at who *I* am. Don't you have a conception of who the right woman for you is?"

"No."

"It's amazing you haven't had a dozen wives," she said, teasing him.

"Maybe, but people are people. You can't design a person for yourself the way you can a living room. Are you actually saying you have a Mr. Right all picked out for yourself?"

"Sort of. It's not *that* rigid."

Chris frowned. "Describe him."

"His physical attributes aren't that critical to me. In fact, somebody like you'd do nicely."

"Thanks a lot."

"You're welcome." She shot him a look and smiled. "It *was* a compliment. Physically. . . well, I'd say we're pretty compatible there so far. But I know women— *and* men—who won't go out with blondes, redheads, brunettes, guys under six feet, women over thirty. You know, silly external stuff."

"So it's the silly internal stuff that makes your Mr. Right right for you?"

"Uh-huh. He would have a strong sense of self."

"Which I do."

"Definitely. He would also not have the kind of so-called male ego that would object to a woman who didn't need to be supported financially."

"Comes under strong sense of self, I would think."

"So would I. He would also have a certain degree of sophistication."

Chris leaned back and polished off the last of his beer. "Does a view of the Public Garden from his messy desk count?"

"Maybe. My definition of sophistication has changed over the years. I used to think it meant dining regularly at the Ritz, but now I'm more inclined to think it means being at ease dining at the Ritz—or anywhere else, for that matter. It's a small but critical distinction."

"We're back to a strong sense of self again. Someone who doesn't have anything to prove can feel comfortable at the Ritz or at a greasy spoon."

"I agree."

"So what's Mr. Right do for a living?"

"He's neither a parasite nor a shark."

"That doesn't leave much, you know. What about what I do?"

She almost choked. "You're not serious."

"Shark?"

"Of the great white school."

He grinned. "Good. I'd hate to do what I do and be a damn jellyfish, and I sure as hell don't want to be accused of being a tapeworm of society. I like shark. Does this Mr. Right have to make more money than you do?"

"Absolutely not. He doesn't have to make much money at all, as long as he's happy in his work."

"And doesn't object when you pay for the bill at the Ritz. Okay." He digested that and looked at her thoughtfully, but she wasn't sure just how seriously he was taking her. "Tell me more about this Mr. Right. He's okay looking, he's not a jackass, he doesn't call caviar fish eggs, he doesn't mind eating home fries and he makes money by enlightening mankind. What else?"

She regarded him coolly. "You're making fun of me."

"No, I'm not. I'm making fun of Mr. Right. I'm jealous of him. He's sitting there inside your brain, and I'm sitting over here on this couch all by myself. What else does this guy have going for him that I don't? A clean office?"

"Not necessarily, but he has his priorities straight, and he's self-disciplined and self-motivated."

"He *would* have a clean refrigerator."

"Let's put it this way. If we shared an apartment, he would accept that a clean refrigerator is one of my priorities and wouldn't object to helping keep it clean."

"So long as you tolerated his messy office."

"I suppose some arrangement could be made."

"I guess the hell it could since this guy's a saint, anyway. He'd probably offer to clean the fridge every night after supper just to have the chance to live with you. But you've never really given much thought about things like clean refrigerators and overcrowded coat trees and finding his hairs in the sink, have you?"

"No, but . . ."

"And you want to know why?" Chris leaned forward, his slate eyes riveted on her. He thumped the arm of the couch with one finger. *"Because this guy doesn't exist!"*

Page refused to respond emotionally. "I'm not saying he does." Her tone was objective and logical. "I'm just saying these are the qualities I'd always expected to find in the man I fell in love with."

"Does this Mr. Right worship you?"

"I don't want worship. But he'd make me feel like no other man alive does."

"That's the key, isn't it?" Chris was so close to her he could have touched her knee, but he didn't. "Someone who makes you feel like no one else can—"

"No!" She shook her head firmly. "Compatibility is the key. When all the fire and fury wear off, you have to be able to get along with that person."

"Who says the 'fire and fury' will ever wear off? I'm not saying compatibility's not important. It is. But you don't fall in love with an extension of yourself. You don't fall in love with some guy you've made up. You fall in love with a person with good points and bad points. Dammit, you don't wait around for some Mr. Right who doesn't exist. You fall in love with someone who's right for you—and someone for whom *you're* right. Loving's important, too, not just being loved."

She stared at him, struck by the passion with which he spoke as much as the words themselves. "And I was convinced you'd just laugh at me."

"Laugh? Hell, lady, I've never had to compete with thin air before. No laughing matter as far as I'm concerned."

She bit back a smile. "You know what I'm saying, don't you?"

It wasn't really a question: she already knew he did. But he grinned and straightened. "Yeah, I guess. I don't fit your preconceptions of the guy who's going to get you."

"Right. And you *do* fit into my family—which is another problem."

"Problem? Why can't that be one point in my favor!"

"Well, it is and it isn't."

"Aha. Mr. Right wouldn't fit. Hell, no. He'd never fix fences and haul sap and chop wood with Grandpa, and he'd sure as the devil never eat chili and corn bread with that crowd you call a family. Page, you know what?"

She shook her head.

"You make me crazy."

"I guess I must."

"That's okay. It keeps me on edge."

"And it's different, isn't it?"

He frowned. "What?"

"I'm not what you're used to. I'm different."

"That you are, Page B. No question about it. You're different. But if you're thinking this weekend was just a whim on my part because you're not the kind of woman I usually go for, you're wrong." He got up and picked up her hands from her lap and lifted her to her feet, then slipped his hands around her waist. "I'm not going to try to be Mr. Right. I'm going to be me. And if that's not good enough, if that's not what you want or what you need, you're going to have to figure that out for yourself and tell me so. But what I am is what you get. It's all I can give."

"I guess that's all anyone can ask." She pulled his hands from her waist and winced when she glanced at her watch. "I hate to say this, and I know my timing's bad, but I've got to head home."

He smiled and kissed her lightly on the lips. "You couldn't be persuaded to stay?"

"Oh, I probably could—"

"But you'd hate me in the morning when you had to sneak across the Public Garden at dawn with your teeth not brushed. Always so practical."

She laughed. "That about sums it up."

"You're sure it's not the prospect of spending the night in a disorganized household?"

"Don't be silly. Of course not."

"I'd go back to your place with you, but I'm afraid I've got to burn the midnight oil to meet a deadline tomorrow."

"Such responsibility."

"Such idiocy," he said, and kissed her hard.

CHRIS GOT HER OUT of his apartment fast before he could say to hell with responsibility and practicality and whisk Page B. off to his bedroom. He could get up early and finish his column, and there had to be a fresh toothbrush kicking around his apartment somewhere. But he didn't work well first thing in the morning. And Page could have managed if she'd wanted to. The problem was she was afraid to make the effort. Afraid to need him too much. Afraid to make him an integral part of her life. Afraid to make him fit. From what he'd seen of her family, he could guess she'd fought hard to make herself stable and organized—and she was scared to death he was going to erase all her gains and throw her back into chaos.

And he supposed he didn't blame her, because, dammit, he just might. He measured his control over his life by its degree of spontaneity. She measured her control over her life by its degree of predictability.

"T'ain't no way to reconcile the two," he muttered.

But what the hell. They'd have to figure something out. They *belonged* together. Now that he had a taste of Page B. Harrington in his life, there was no way he could go on without her.

The rest was more or less just a question of logistics.

Or so he told himself as he pulled out the chair to his desk and got to work.

FORTY MINUTES LATER Page pressed Chris's buzzer for the third time, growing impatient. He had to be up; she'd seen the light in his attic window. Had he nodded off? Was he so absorbed in his work he didn't hear the buzzer? Was the damn buzzer *broken*?

She marched out to the sidewalk and craned her neck as she peered up at the window. It was open. "Chris?" she called, not very loudly.

No answer.

"Chris."

Still nothing.

She cleared her throat and glanced around for anyone looking, and then tried once more in a loud hiss. "Chris!"

Nothing.

Obviously he was going to have her reduced to throwing stones again! She started looking around for something to pitch up to his window to get his attention. There was another bit of brick over there and . . . *What was she doing?*

She grabbed the brick chip, which fit handily into her palm, and checked up and down the street for any police.

Then she heaved the brick up as high and hard as she could and—

Crack!

Her aim was right on target this time. A little too right on target. The brick had struck the glass upper part of the attic window rather than the screen.

Up in the attic she could hear a curse and the window being yanked open. She ducked behind a shrub in the tiny space that passed for a front yard; at least she was out of view of the upstairs.

"What the hell's going on down there?"

Chris sounded annoyed. She didn't blame him: she'd cracked his damn window. She was debating whether to 'fess up or just sneak back to her apartment, when she heard the window bang shut.

Then she heard the pounding of feet on the stairs inside the building. It sounded as if he were taking them three and four at a time, which indeed was apparently the case, because in a matter of half a minute he landed breathless and fuming on the sidewalk in front of her shrub. His hands were on his hips and his eyes were narrowed as he scanned the sidewalk for the offender—who was perhaps eighteen inches behind him. Page didn't breathe.

He turned and spotted her. "You!"

"Well, hello, there." She stepped guiltily from behind the shrub and ran one hand through her hair. "I thought I spotted a discarded quarter under this shrub here. You know me. Waste not, want not."

"*You* broke my window?"

"Broke your— No, of course not. I just got here. I did notice three or four teenagers racing up Beacon as I arrived. They cut down Charles."

He crossed his arms over his chest. "Liar."

"Me? Lie?"

"Organized people lie better than the rest of us. They have a knack for sorting out whatever mess they happen to find themselves in and finding the most workable situation. You, Page B., are the most organized person I know and therefore the biggest liar."

"That's a generalization. It's also not true."

He held his palm out to her. "The quarter."

"It wasn't there. A trick of the light, I think."

"Quick, Page B. Real quick. How do you keep coming up with them?"

"Don't you want to know what I've been up to?"

He raised his chin and looked down his straight nose at her. "You've been throwing rocks at my window—"

"It was a brick and I only threw one."

"A brick!"

"Just a piece of one. Good aim, huh?"

"You planned it that way, I suppose."

"Nope. I just winged it. And see what happened?"

"You broke my damn window."

"I got your attention. If you'd answered your buzzer, this wouldn't have happened."

"Blame it on me. I didn't hear the buzzer."

"Why not?"

"It's broken."

She sighed, shaking her head. "Not that line again."

"It's true. Broke the other day. You must be a jinx or something. I should make you fix it and the window."

"I didn't do a thing to your buzzer! And it's not my fault I broke your window. If you'd had your buzzer fixed, you'd have heard me and answered your door like a civilized human being, instead of forcing me to throw a brick to get your attention."

"Wait just a minute—"

"But I'm willing to call us even. You fix your buzzer and your window yourself, and I'll forgive you for putting me through such trauma. Anyway, don't you want to know what I'm doing back here?"

"Looking for quarters," he muttered.

"Uh-uh." She held up the small overnight case she held in one hand. "I brought my toothbrush."

11

ON A WEDNESDAY AFTERNOON two weeks later, Chris had his feet up on his desk and was looking out across the Public Garden, where the grass had turned green and the leaves were budding. Spring had arrived in full force; he hardly ever had to close his window now. But the feel of the warm breeze on his face only made him want Page. He'd like to whisk her away for the afternoon—walk the Freedom Trail, eat hot dogs off a cart, take a ride up the coast, make love to her in the fresh spring grass. That, however, was impossible. Page was working. Page was responsible. Page was not spontaneous.

He sighed. *And you're being unfair.*

They'd had a spectacular two weeks. They'd driven out to Concord one weekend and met his family, his parents having just returned from Florida. Page had fit right in with her smile and her poise and her knowledge of business. His mother had liked her so much she tried to lure Page into a conspiracy to get rid of her only son's "horrid truck." But Page, laughing afterward with him in bed, had said, "Now I understand why you're so disorganized. You were brought up with very rigid ideas about what it means to be responsible, organized and all that. To establish your independence, you rebelled against what essentially were artificial expectations."

"Whatever," he said. At the time talk was the last thing on his mind.

"It's your determination and goal-oriented nature that counts. You *are* responsible, but in your own way."

"Uh-huh." He'd taken a pink nipple between his fingers and begun rubbing it gently, erotically, to shut her up.

It hadn't. At least not right away. "But don't worry—I'd never try to reform you!"

She liked him just the way he was. And now that had him worried.

If their relationship was going to grow, he'd have to make compromises. As much as she enjoyed his bed, she could barely tolerate how he lived. It drove her nuts when he tossed the morning newspaper on the floor beside the bed and ate cold pizza for breakfast. His capacity for spontaneity thrilled her—and unnerved her, too. He knew she felt out of control, a little crazy.

But he wasn't going to pretend he could change completely. He couldn't. He could no more drop into her organized life than she could drop into his disorganized life. Her 4:15 message checks and mail-sorting routine drove *him* nuts. He found her schedules constricting. He couldn't live her life. She couldn't live his. Did that mean they couldn't build some kind of life together?

No. It couldn't. Somehow he'd do a little giving and she'd do a little giving and they'd work something out. They *had* to.

The telephone rang, and he seized it, thinking it might be Page. Maybe she'd been staring out her window and wanted to get out. But when William Norton said hello, Chris told himself he should have known better: Page had a business to maintain. Obligations. Different from his, but as important. If he took off for an afternoon, he could always make up for it that night. She couldn't, especially when she had a client. As it was, her filing was backed up after he'd spirited her away from a "filing session" to join Millie and William for a rare weekday afternoon Red Sox game.

"What's up, William?"

"I've got news."

He sounded excited—and nervous. "What's that?"

William hesitated.

Chris leaned over his grandfather's typewriter and felt his heart race. "Bill? Is something wrong?"

"No. No, everything's great. It's good news. I . . . Millie and I are getting married."

PAGE HAD HAD DIFFICULTY concentrating all afternoon and was relieved when she checked her messages at 4:15 to hear Millie Friedenbach's voice. Millie would restore her sense of duty and responsibility and end the disquieting suspicion that Chris had been trying to connect with her telepathically—or *somehow*—to quit early and ride the swan boats in the Public Garden with him.

"Hey, Page," Millie's cheerful voice said on the message machine, "by dinner tomorrow night William and I'll be married. Think I should keep my own name?"

That was it. No explanation, no details. Page almost choked. What was Millie up to *this* time? She tried her best friend's apartment six times before she finally gave up and called Chris.

"You've heard?" she asked.

"'Bout what?"

"Millie and William."

"Oh, yeah. William called about an hour ago and told me he and Millie are getting married tomorrow."

"And what are you doing?"

"Working on my column."

"*What!* How can you concentrate?"

"It's not easy. I keep thinking about you."

"Never mind *me*. What about William and Millie? How can you possibly work when you know by this time tomorrow those two are going to be married? We've got to do something!"

"Why?"

"They've known each other less time than we have!"

"And William says they'd spent virtually every minute of their days together and he's come to know her as he never knew his ex-wife, to whom, I might add, he was married seven years."

Page groaned. "You gave him your blessing?"

"Sure."

"You think I'm overreacting." It wasn't an accusation: she wasn't sure herself she wasn't overreacting.

"Right again."

"You don't know Millie. She's liable to do anything—and half of what she does she regrets later. I can't just stand by and let her make a mistake. I'm her *friend*."

"Who says she *is* making a mistake? Page, William's a good guy. And he's in love with her."

"What if they're out of control?"

"What they are is on their way to Florida. They're getting married by a justice of the peace and then taking Beth to Disney World for their honeymoon."

"But Millie has to work."

"She had some personal time coming."

"What about Beth's school?"

"She's in the first grade, Page. What she misses won't hurt her for life—and her mom's getting married, right? That and Disney World ought to make up for missing a couple of days of school."

Page forced herself to sit down at the kitchen table and calm down. But didn't the man see her point? "And William would have no trouble taking a week or two off now—"

"Now that you've organized him," Chris finished for her.

She sighed miserably. "It's all my fault. I knew Millie would do anything for hockey tickets, but I never thought . . . well, they just didn't seem a pair. Do you know what I mean? There are no checks and balances where they're concerned. They're both incurable romantics and unbelievably impulsive and disorganized. Qualities like that lead to . . . to Disney World marriages!"

"To each his or her own. I've got the name of the place they're staying. We can send them flowers."

"You're not worried?"

"Sure I'm worried, but they're adults. They can make their own decisions."

"Millie's my best friend."

"How do you plan to stop her? They've already left. William was calling me from the airport. You can't very well go to Florida and talk them out of it."

Page didn't respond immediately. Florida. If she could get an early flight, she could be there by mid-morning, or noon at the latest, and take a late flight back.

"Page?"

"I'm thinking."

"Page—"

"I'll call you back in fifteen minutes."

"*Page!*"

She hung up and started calling airlines. There were no cheaper fares available, but she could book two first-class seats on a direct flight to Orlando at seven tomorrow morning. It would cost a fortune. Holding her breath, she recited the number of her American Express gold card—she had all her credit card numbers memorized—and booked the two seats.

Her hands were shaking, and she was breathing fast. It took three tries to tap out Chris's number. She sat back and swallowed hard, trying to regain her composure, but Chris answered on the first ring.

"Page, what the hell's going on?"

She told him.

"Are you crazy? You've got work to do tomorrow, remember? You said this morning you couldn't spend the night because you had to be up so early, but now you can go traipsing off to Florida to horn in on your best friend's honeymoon? And me—I've got a deadline."

"I can make arrangements," she said. "And you don't have to come if you don't want to."

"Now who's being impulsive?"

She could almost see his wry smile, and it did things to her insides she couldn't think about right now. "No, I'm being a friend. If I were doing something Millie thought questionable, I'd want her to take action. I...I'm *not* being impulsive, dammit. This is a rational plan based on an objective look at the facts."

"Horse hockey. You're being crazy and I love it. I'll pack my bags and be at your place in an hour."

THEY TOOK A CAB to Logan Airport the next morning. Chris insisted the subway was faster, but Page said a cab was more civilized. She refused to look at him so he could say he told her so when they got caught up in tunnel traffic. But they made the airport in plenty of time for their seven o'clock flight—which was no thanks to one energetic journalist. Since they had to be up so early and didn't have much time to sleep, he'd reasoned, why sleep at all?

She picked up the tickets. "Wait, there's a mistake. I booked a return flight for tonight. These are just one-way tickets."

The efficient-looking woman behind the counter informed her that according to the computer, reservations for the return flight had been canceled. Unfortunately there were no seats available. She checked other flights. "No, nothing until tomorrow, I'm afraid."

"I don't have time for this," Page grumbled, and finally she gave up. She'd deal with the problem of getting out of Florida once she got there. Tucking their tickets in the outer compartment of her pocketbook, she breezed out into the corridor, Chris Battle right beside her. She went on huffily, "Honestly, it's amazing to me airlines *ever* make a profit."

"Maybe they should hire Get It Together Inc."

"Maybe they should! How could they let something like this happen?"

"Impossible to imagine."

"*You* don't seem upset."

He shrugged. "Why waste energy trying to change what I can't change?"

"Well, I *have* to be back for tomorrow. My clients were very decent about my traipsing off to Florida to rescue a friend, but I can't put them off another day."

"What about rescheduling them altogether?"

"Oh, God, no. What a mess that'd be! I'd have to rearrange my entire calendar."

"What do you do when you get sick?"

She sniffed. "I don't get sick."

With that they reached their gate. Chris stepped aside and let Page make all the arrangements for boarding. He'd offered to pay his half of the fare, but she'd turned him down, explaining that since the entire business was her idea, she'd accept full financial responsibility. He'd said fine, but he considered what she paid a hefty amount for a one-way seat to Orlando, Florida.

He'd even quoted her the exact figure.

As she got her boarding pass, Page frowned and thought suddenly, how did he know how much a one-way ticket cost?

CHRIS HAD THE FEELING that Page was onto him, just as she'd been that first day when he'd tried to get her to take him on as a client. She was not an easy woman to hoodwink. But he wasn't ready to explain.

"Chris, buddy, do me a favor. Don't let Page stop us!"

Easy for you to ask, my friend, Chris thought. William, however, *was* his friend, and he'd promised at least to try to keep Page from doing anything as sensible as asking the two lovers if they knew what they were doing.

"If marriage is what they want," she said as she settled into the window seat, "then fine. But I'd like to know if they've considered the consequences of their actions."

"Page, they've both been married before. I think they know."

She scowled at him. "Then why aren't they making *sure* they're doing the right thing in getting married so soon?"

"Maybe they are sure."

"How could they be?"

He looked at her, with her jaw set and her arms crossed. "Don't be so self-righteous. Come on, Page. How sure is sure? When do you know you're doing the right thing? Marriage is a big step, and you shouldn't go into it lightly. But it's always going to be a risk."

"It doesn't have to be as risky as William and Millie are making it. They barely know each other!"

"But they love each other. Isn't that enough?"

"It's a start, but it's not enough."

"You have a timetable for relationships?" he asked dryly.

"Of course not."

"Then tell me. How long do people have to know each other before they should get married?"

She lifted her shoulders and frowned. "Until they're convinced they want to make a lifelong commitment to each other."

"So Millie and William are sure after a few weeks. With other people it takes years."

"As a matter of principle," she said in her organizer's voice, "people shouldn't get married until they've known each other at least a year."

A year! Chris nearly choked.

He decided he'd better not tell Page B. that he had no intention of waiting a whole damn year. First, he thought, he had to resolve the Friedenbach-Norton dilemma.

"'Oh, what a tangled web we weave...'"

Page gave him a sharp look. "Hmm?"

"I was remarking on the view. Boston's spectacular from the air, isn't it?"

PAGE HAD DECIDED to let one Christopher O. Battle cook his own goose.

As she leaned against the counter at the car rental booth, letting him do the honors, she noticed a sexy film of sweat on his neck, just above the rather frayed collar of his chambray shirt. It was warm in Orlando. But not that warm.

The man was up to no good.

"You know where Millie and William are staying?" she asked.

"Yeah... sort of." He shoved the rental receipt in his wallet and grinned at the clerk as he headed off with the key. Page followed. "Some hotel."

"Which? This is Disney country. Vacation land. There must be dozens."

"Uh, we'll figure that out. Come on."

He'd rented an inexpensive compact. Red. Page would have specified a neutral color. She hated red cars. Chris, however, seemed pleased as he patted the hood and said it looked pretty good to him. He unlocked the passenger side for her. "Sure you don't want to drive?"

"Quite," she said. "You're the one who can find Millie."

"Right."

He got in the driver's seat and drove.

When they reached the Bay Hill Country Club, he turned into a vacant driveway. "Missed my turn," he said.

"Do you know where you're going?" she asked dubiously.

"Sure."

"I don't see any hotels. How far are we from Disney World?"

"About thirty miles, I think."

Millie Friedenbach would never stay thirty miles from anywhere. Page could almost hear her friend: "I'd have to listen to Beth yammering all the way to Disney World about Mickey Mouse and Donald Duck. If I'm going to Disney World, I'm going to stay as close to Goofy and company as I can."

Page had never been to Disney World, but she understood there were hotels within the amusement park grounds. That was where Millie would be.

If she was in Florida, which Page was beginning to think was questionable.

What the devil was Battle up to this time?

The car air-conditioning worked perfectly—certainly *she* wasn't sweating—but he had perspiration stains in his armpits now, as well. He was a hot-blooded male, and she reveled in the feel of the film of perspiration on his back after they'd made love. But this was different. This was *guilt* sweat.

"Are you sure we're not lost?" she asked.

"Yep. Just missed my turn, is all."

"Would you like me to look for a sign?"

"Uh-uh."

Because there was no sign, just a road. A dirt road at that. It was barely a car's width and disappeared into an orange grove. Chris turned off the air-conditioning and rolled down his window, and Page did the same. They could smell the sweet smell of the trees, apparently just coming back after the bad freezes of the past few years.

"This isn't a hotel," Page said.

"Oh . . . did you think we were going to a hotel?"

"Chris . . ."

"My mind must have been elsewhere. I haven't been out here in a while."

Page frowned. "Out where?"

Chris turned to her and grinned, a wide, sexy, unabashed grin. "Do I detect a note of doubt in your tone?"

They bumped over a series of ruts; the citrus trees were so close she could have reached out and pulled off the glossy green leaves. Page leaned her head back against the seat. All she wanted was to breathe in the fresh, scented air. Why not just roll with Chris and his latest nefarious scheme?

"Where are you taking me?" she asked.

"Here," he said as they came to a wide clearing in the middle of the grove.

A pink stucco cottage of Old Florida vintage with pink and red and yellow roses climbing on its open porch stood at one side of the clearing. Beyond it was a huge lawn of rich green grass and fat cedar trees and, along the tiny lake at the opposite edge of the grove, weeping willows. A huge yellow cat lay stretching in the sun on a picnic table.

Chris turned to Page and brushed her cheek with the back of his hand. "Well, darling," he said, any look of guilt gone, "welcome to heaven."

THE LIGHT SCENT of the roses and the pungent scent of the freshly mowed grass overpowered Page as she followed Chris toward the cottage, and she felt that strange fullness of unfocused emotion. She was reminded of how orderly her life had been before Christopher O. Battle had blundered into it. How steady her routines. How stable she'd felt. There had been those occasional flirtations with spring fever, but the first warm days after a long winter could do that to anyone. She'd had such control over her life.

Now she was in Florida, which wasn't exactly her own doing, and she was smelling roses and fresh grass and feeling the warmth of the sun on the back of her neck. And she was thinking heaven should be as beautiful as this place. And hearing herself sigh. And brushing her fingertips across the petals of a perfect pink rose blossom and feeling her insides swell with a motley of emotions.

In the groves surrounding the cottage birds twittered.

Don't let yourself be seduced by flowers and birds!

Calling upon all her considerable powers of self-discipline, she drew herself up straight and inhaled sharply and deeply. She refused to smell anything but a rat.

Said rat was whistling a tune as he found a key under a flower pot and unlocked the back door to the cottage, his shirt, Page noticed with satisfaction, matted to his back. All appearances aside, he *didn't* know how she'd reacted to being tricked: she had yet to say a word about his "heaven."

Let him roast, she thought.

But the roses and the warmth accosted her senses once more, and she had to stiffen her spine and will herself to maintain her sense of outrage. Chris had manipulated her.

He glanced over his shoulder as she followed him into the kitchen. "Cute little place, isn't it?"

"Adorable."

She was being curt, but not inaccurate. The kitchen was old-fashioned and painted white, with cheerful yellow curtains and tablecloth and open shelves stacked with simple white dishes. There were no fancy appliances: a clear glass percolator stood on the stove, and a dented aluminum dishpan hung on a hook by the sink. Page could feel all the starch in her turning to sop as the infectious charm of the place took its toll.

Chris opened the refrigerator, half humming, half whistling. "Aha! Look what we have here. Perfection!"

He seized a pitcher of fresh-squeezed orange juice and set it on the countertop while he got down two glasses and proceeded to fill them. Page didn't offer to help. She stood awkwardly by the table and kept telling herself that she'd been tricked and her nostrils ought to be filled with rat odors and her heart with outrage. But all she could think about was the feel of that cold orange juice coursing down her throat and the joy of being in this lovely place alone with Chris.

He handed her a glass. "We'll sit out on the porch and relax a minute. How's that?"

"Fine." Page gritted her teeth against the emotions churning inside her, as if that would help to keep them locked in. "Um, whose place is this?"

"Fellow by the name of Lawrence Cutter."

"Friend of yours?"

"Yep. He writes for the Orlando paper."

"Where is he?"

"On his way to Boston, I expect."

Chris took a sip of orange juice and headed down a gleaming oak-floored hall to the front porch. He plopped down on a slatted swing. Page settled her bottom on the flat rail of the porch—a dangerous move. The smell of roses surrounded her; it was nearly impossible to smell a rat.

Leaning back, Chris looked at ease. Smug, even. Too at ease, too smug. As if he'd already gotten away with whatever it was he was up to.

Which Page had a sneaking suspicion he had.

"Why's this friend of yours going to Boston?" she asked. She decided she'd hang him one question at a time.

"Research for an article he's decided to write."

"On what?"

"On Boston."

"That's rather vague. Has he been planning to write this article for very long?"

He gave the swing a little push with his feet. "Well, he's always wanted to go to Boston."

"Why now?"

"Because I made him an offer he couldn't refuse."

Naturally. "Which was?"

"A week at my place on Beacon Hill in exchange for a week at his place here. You know how much a week at the Four Seasons costs?"

"There are more inexpensive hotels. When did you make this deal?"

He stuck out his toe and stopped the swing, his slate eyes lost in the shadows on the porch. "About three minutes after you called yesterday afternoon."

Page said nothing.

"It seemed like a propitious moment. Lawrence was thrilled. Turned out his wife had some time coming to her at her job and could go with him. They're making it sort of a second honeymoon."

"How nice," Page said.

Chris unbuttoned his shirt and pulled it off, then balled it up and cast it on the white-painted floor. He sat there in his sweaty white undershirt. Page noticed the dark hairs poking out along the neckline and looked away.

She asked, "Then you're planning to stay here a week?"

"Sure. Why not?"

"You didn't bring any luggage."

He shrugged. "If I had, you'd have gotten suspicious."

"I already *was* suspicious!" But she calmed herself down; there was no point in losing control until she had all the facts. "What about Millie and William?"

"They're not here."

She balled her hands into fists and kicked the rail. "Dammit, I know they're not here!" She tried to rein in her emotions but couldn't as she glared at Chris, who seemed pleased by her fast-ebbing control, as if she wasn't quite so tightly wound as he sometimes imagined. "Where the hell are they?"

"Bermuda."

"*Bermuda!*"

Chris nodded. "I'm to distract you long enough for them to get married in peace."

"What's that supposed to mean?"

"It means, darling, that they adore you and appreciate your friendship and your thoughtfulness—but they don't want you trying to talk them out of getting married."

She said nothing, the impact of his words hitting her hard. Her friends didn't want her meddling. That was what Chris was saying.

"They knew your first impulse would be to stop them," he added, his smooth tone more merciless than angry. "I know you think they're out of control, but who isn't when they're in love?"

He had a point, but she said, "They don't trust me."

"Of course they trust you. But they also know you. Their deepest romantic fantasy has been to fall madly in love and sneak off to some paradise island and get married. All right, so 'reality' has bumped and bruised them. So they've both been divorced and Millie has a six-year-old daughter. They know they're not kids. But they know what they want. They've learned from their mistakes, and they know they can't go through life being afraid to make new ones."

"I just wanted to be sure . . ."

"For their sake or for yours?"

She inhaled deeply and suddenly couldn't answer, couldn't think. Swinging her legs over the rail, she jumped into the soft grass and fled across the lawn to the edge of the tiny lake. She had to pull herself together! What did all this mean? Were Millie and William trying to tell her anything?

Yes, she thought. That they knew her just as well as she prided herself in knowing them.

She felt Chris's presence behind her and was relieved when he didn't touch her. Physical contact now would only further confuse her—and distract her. She didn't turn around but looked out across the still lake.

"I'm not just a meddler," she said, half to herself.

"I know."

"I tried to explain to you the first day we met that my goal always is to help people better understand themselves and work with what they have—not always with what they want, what they dream of getting, what they always believe will be around the next corner."

"There's nothing wrong with that," Chris said. "Part of your success lies in your ability to accept people's differences, their peculiarities, what makes *them* tick. You don't impose your values and systems on them."

"I'm not a fraud."

"Of course not. Millie and William know that—and so do I."

"Then why are they in Bermuda and I'm in Florida?"

Chris came and stood beside her. "Because you're the victim of a nefarious plot."

"Because my own impulsiveness clouded my judgment! I should have stepped back outside of myself a minute and figured out what was going on."

"Page B., you're allowed."

"Allowed what? A chance to make an ass of myself?"

"A chance to dream," he said. "A chance to blow with the wind like everyone else. You don't always have to be in control. You *can't* be. No one can. I should have told you what was going on last night, but I . . . well, I couldn't resist. It was a chance to try to do you one up again. I was having a good time. I forgot that you might not appreciate being decoyed off to Florida." He tried a grin on her. "You have to admit you fell for everything I said without even considering I might be . . ." He fumbled for the right word.

Page supplied one. "Lying?"

"I prefer . . . 'strategizing.'"

She sighed, squinting at the sun. She'd need a hat if she was going to stay here for a while. But she stiffened at the thought, feeling a wave of panic. *I can't stay!* Was she beyond help even to consider that she could?

"All I wanted was to help my friends."

"Page, you don't always have to have all the answers. Some things don't have answers. Whether Millie and William should get married is one of them. *Why* they're in love is another."

"You know," she said, looking out at the lake as a fish jumped and disappeared, leaving behind a pattern of concentric circles. It was so quiet here. Heaven, she thought. "When you quoted the ticket prices at Logan, I knew you were the one who'd canceled our return flight. I *knew* you were up to something, and I didn't stop you. I— Dammit, I don't know what got into me! And now Millie and William . . ."

"Are in Bermuda having a hell of a time."

"Knowing them, I'd say so."

"You've done too much to help them for either to ever resent you. They accept you for who you are. Accept them for who they are."

"I do!"

"Then you'll toast them with champagne at four o'clock when they exchange their vows? William asked us to."

She glanced at him, a maniacal smile on her face. "Think we could make Bermuda by four?"

His eyes darkened. "Page B...."

"I'm kidding." She laughed, then slipped an arm around his waist. "You're all sweaty."

"Can't imagine why. I've been expecting you to nail me to the wall ever since I cooked up this scheme."

"What happens now?"

He put his arm around her, too. "We make the best of the situation."

"I figured you'd say something like that. How're we supposed to get back to Boston? We have no return tickets."

"Sure we do."

"We do?"

"For next Wednesday."

"*Wednesday!* But that's a whole week from now! My work—"

"Your work will not suffer. You told me yourself you had a lull so you could take a couple of days off to 're-group'—an organizer's phrase if I've ever heard one—and catch up on some busywork in your office and work on a book on getting organized. I'm sure you can buy notebooks in Florida and set your things up on the porch and work on your book. That's exactly where I intend to write my next column, which I will dutifully call in to my editor. 'Busywork' implies something that can wait. So let it wait. And if you can't 'regroup' here, where the hell can you?"

She sighed, her uneasiness dissipating, giving way to the feeling of warmth and excitement of being with him. "You can be persuasive, you know."

He laughed. "Why do you think I'm nationally syndicated?"

"We have no luggage."

His arm edged higher up her side and stopped just under her breast. "Who needs clothes?"

"You *are* a rat."

"Have you ever made love in the grass?" he asked, swinging her around in front of him and bringing his mouth close to hers.

"There might be alligators in that lake," she said, settling her hands on his chest. "And the soil's pretty sandy. What if we land on a mound of little bitty black ants that'll bite your behind?"

"Or worse," he added with a shudder. "Always so practical."

"But it'd be a shame to waste this beautiful day. I did notice a wicker lounge on the porch . . ."

"Sometimes, my darling, we do think alike."

THE COUCH WAS COVERED in pink chintz and not terribly wide. If they rolled one way, Page reckoned, they'd hit the prickly wicker back. If they rolled the other way, they'd fall on the floor. And if anyone drove up the long driveway, they'd be caught.

"The bedroom?" Chris asked.

Page bit her lower lip. "Well . . . if anyone *does* drive up, we'll hear them long before they get here. And I've never made love on a wicker lounge. I mean, it's not like we're going to be attacked by ants or alligators. Unexpected company and ending up on the floor aren't big risks, but they'd lend a certain thrill to the proceedings, don't you think?"

He quirked a brow at her. "Proceedings?"

"You know. Lovemaking."

"I know, dammit. Do you analyze *everything*?"

"Well, if you'd prefer the bedroom..."

"What I prefer is you."

And he stuck his foot out and gave the side of her foot a little kick that knocked her off balance, sending her sprawling down onto the couch. Laughing, she thrust out one leg, hooked it around his knees and brought him down on top of her. She shivered at the salty, sexy smell of him.

"You've got me," she said.

He responded with a low growl as his mouth came down on hers, his tongue opening her lips and plunging in with a heat that could match any Florida produced. His hands slipped between their bodies and attacked the buttons on her blouse, wrinkled from the plane and the heat. In seconds he'd dispensed with the blouse and her bra, and her breasts felt full and swollen in the outdoor warmth. He pulled back, his gaze lingering on her pink nipples, and he brought his head down toward them, holding back for what seemed an eternity, until his tongue flicked out, wet and hot against first one nipple, then the other.

"I've thought about this moment all day," he said, grabbing at the waist of her skirt and pushing it down, until finally he had to tackle the clasp. "On the plane...I could have made love to you in the damn aisle."

His words further imflamed her, and she helped with the skirt and the underpants and stockings, then with his garments, until they were naked in the spring air, their smooth bodies coming together on the limited space of the couch. A breeze tickled her sensitized skin, and she straddled his hips as, with fingers splayed, her hands trailed over every inch of his torso, up his neck and jaw. He nibbled on the tips of her fingers.

And he raised her above him and lowered her slowly, erotically, onto him.

She held back a cry and listened instead to his. Felt him thrust himself deeper into her. Felt his hips arch as he realized her game. "Think you can stay still, do you?" he said in a guttural whisper, and he grinned, seizing her breasts in his palms. "We'll see . . ."

With his thumbs he traced the outline of her nipples, then, first with tiny circles, then larger and larger circles, took in all over the soft swell of her breasts. She had to bite her lower lip to keep on with her game.

"You feel so good," he murmured, "so right."

He smoothed his hands down her sides to her bottom and, lifting her slightly off him, brought her down quick and hard. She gasped. So much for any game! She could hold back her aching desire no longer and responded with an urgency that matched his.

When they were spent, exhausted and fulfilled, she collapsed on him and exulted in the scent of grass and roses and the cooling breeze on her overheated skin.

"I never want to move," she said, her breathing beginning to return to normal. "I just want to lie here forever."

"Same here . . ."

"But you know, my level of risk tolerance can only take so much abuse. Do you keep hearing a car?"

"Uh-uh."

"Neither do I. But I keep thinking I might start hearing one any second."

So they got their wrinkled clothes back on. Page commented that they'd have to make a trip to the store; *she* wasn't going to wear her things another day.

"I suppose these friends of yours don't have a washer and dryer?"

"Nope. Washtub and clothesline."

"Well, *I* don't intend to wash out my underwear in the sink every night. There must be a store close by."

"Several, I'm sure. This is the booming Sunshine State."

"If you'd only *told* me . . ."

"If I'd told you, you'd never have come."

"Well . . ."

She was going to leave it at that, but he prodded her. "True or false?"

"Doesn't matter. It's a moot point. I'm here."

He relented and headed inside for cold drinks. Feeling almost limp with relaxation, Page sat on the swing and gave herself a push.

Heaven . . .

Chris returned with two tall glasses of fresh-squeezed lemonade and handed her one. "Marry me," he said.

She blinked at him. *"What?"*

He grinned and sat beside her in the swing. "Don't have a heart attack on me."

"I'm not . . . I . . . were you serious?"

"Was and am."

She tried the tangy lemonade and rested her head back against his arm, flung across the back of the swing. Marriage. The ultimate commitment.

"I love you, you know," he said.

"Thank you."

"You're thanking me?"

"Well, yes, I mean...well, why not? I'm glad you love me. I love you, too."

"I figured I'd just spring the emotional stuff on you. I know you're not comfortable with a lot of what your little nieces and nephews would call 'mushy talk.' But I do love you and I'm not afraid to say it. I'll climb on top of the roof and crow it to anyone who'll listen. *I love Page B. Harrington and I don't care that I don't know what the B stands for!*"

She was laughing. "You're outrageous."

"Yeah, and you love it. We're the perfect foils for each other. So let's get married and fight and love and laugh together for the rest of our lives."

"You're serious, aren't you?"

He drank some lemonade, the glass hiding much of his expression. But his eyes, dark and frank, stared into hers. "Never more serious."

"When?"

"While we're in Florida. We'll fetch a justice of the peace out here and get married among the rosebushes. Romantic, don't you think?"

"I can't...I mean, my family, my friends— What would your mother say?"

"Hallelujah, probably."

"But..."

"Page, if you have to say no, say it. For God's sake, don't torture me. If you can't stand the thought of marrying me, then—" He inhaled sharply. "Then we'll just have to work out another way of being together. I can't stand the thought of losing you. So don't panic. If you say no—"

"You know, for Boston's wittiest, nastiest journalist, you can be awfully thickheaded sometimes. I'm *not* talking about saying no. I'm talking about the wedding ceremony. I just . . . well, it would feel too impulsive getting married down here. What would I tell my clients?"

Chris's eyes narrowed. "You want an organized wedding."

"Uh-huh."

"But you *do* want a wedding."

Her mind spun with a thousand thoughts, images, sensations and a million hopes and dreams. Marriage . . . Chris in her life forever . . . a different kind of stability than what she had now . . . children . . . a life and a future to share. She closed her eyes and just floated along with all the possibilities.

"Page?"

"It feels so right," she breathed. "I never thought it'd feel this right."

"What does, love?"

"Getting married. Somehow I thought I'd be losing my stability and my sense of responsibility for myself, my independence."

She turned and smiled at him, and realized the strange emotions of the past weeks weren't unfocused, only new. They were the emotions that came with the kind of permanent, lasting, overpowering love she felt for this witty, caring, messy, determined man. She'd never before experienced the sheer strength of such emotion.

"As it so happens," she said, "I can't think of a greater act of independence than falling in love. After all, no one else can do it for you. But the wedding itself . . . well, there are things to be worked out."

"Like what?" Chris asked, his tone filled with challenge and happiness.

"Invitations, my dress, bridesmaids, tracking down my father in Arizona, giving my mother and the rest of the family *plenty* of notice so they can be ready . . . you know. I've always wanted a nice big traditional wedding. It'll take time to organize."

Chris groaned. "How much time?"

"Months. Eight at least. Maybe a year. It'll probably take us that long to work out living arrangements. I mean, there's no *way* I can live in that attic of yours, and I know you're not the fancy condo type, which leaves figuring out something else entirely or fighting out what goes and what stays from each of our assorted junk piles."

"You don't have any junk," Chris grumbled.

"Oh, I do. I'm a pack rat of the first order, just like you. I've got junk stuffed *everywhere*." She grinned at him, feeling excited, renewed. "I'm just an organized pack rat."

"Page . . ."

"Admit it. You know this is all going to take time to work out."

"The hell it is." He reached into his back pocket and pulled out a book of matches. "You set fire to your place, and I'll set fire to mine. We'll start all over again fresh."

She opened her mouth to start a lecture on the lack of wisdom of his proposed idea, but he cut her off with a guffaw that told her he'd gotten her again. With an impulsiveness that was getting to be entirely too much like her, she grabbed an ice cube out of her glass and dumped it down his back . . . and fled.

He caught up with her somewhere in the orange grove, and after that it was their battered clothes and the threat of alligators and little bitty black ants that was damned. Nothing could stop them from making love in the soft grass under an orange tree, and nothing did.

Epilogue

THEY LASTED until September and were married Page's way, at the stark white New England church on the town common near her family's place. The reception afterward was at a Yankee inn with the entire Harrington-Tucker clan there, including Page's father from Arizona. Everyone behaved, except two-year-old Timothy, who stuck his fingers in the billows of wedding cake frosting. But it was Chris's parents who laughed harder than anyone.

They honeymooned Chris's way, with a packed car waiting for them at the inn. They'd both arranged to take off an entire month, but that was all they arranged. They decided to wing the rest, just go where they felt like going and be free and unrestrained as their love. Page didn't even mention things like hotel reservations.

While they were gone, contractors would get to work on the roomy but bedraggled Back Bay town house they'd purchased from the sale of her Four Seasons condominium and his Beacon Street attic. He'd have another attic, she another office, they a master bedroom with two bathrooms and two closets. She would put up with his sweat clothes on the doorknob; he'd put the spatulas back where he got them. They would compromise with each other and, most of all, complement each other.

But there was still the matter of the coat tree.

Chris grinned at her as he started the car, a sporty sedan they'd bought together. "The coat tree stays."

"It's an eyesore," she countered.

"No arguing on our honeymoon."

"Fine. Get rid of the coat tree."

"You have to admit it's convenient."

"It's ugly."

He sighed. They'd covered the same ground a hundred times during the past weeks. "What if I polished it up a bit?"

"It goes in the Dumpster first thing when we get back. Unless—"

She paused, a compromise just having occurred to her. "Well, I suppose I could tolerate it at the back entrance."

"What? Where the devil did you think I wanted to put it?"

"In the front hall."

"What, that eyesore in our front hall! No, no, I meant all along for it to go in the back hall."

"We've been arguing over nothing?"

"So it would seem."

She laughed. "Then everything's settled, and we'll have a grand honeymoon."

"Uh-uh. There's one more thing."

"What? After the sweat clothes on the doorknob and the coat tree, what else can there be?"

"The *B.*"

"What bee?"

"In Page B. Harrington. *Does* it stand for Barracuda?"

"First you tell me what the *O* in Christopher O. Battle stands for."

"You don't expect me to trust you, do you?"

"Actually, no. There are, dear, some things even spouses aren't to know."

SOMETIME AFTER DAWN in an unremarkable inn on the southern coast of Maine, Page rolled over and whispered in Chris's ear, "Beulah."

He didn't laugh. He just turned onto his stomach and said, "Obadiah."

Harlequin Temptation

COMING NEXT MONTH

Harlequin Temptation dares to be different!

Once in a while, we Temptation editors spot a romance that's truly innovative. To make sure *you* don't miss any one of these outstanding selections, we'll mark them for you.

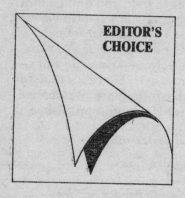

EDITOR'S CHOICE

When the "Editors' Choice" fold-back appears on a Temptation cover, you'll know we've found that extra-special page-turner!

THE

Temptation

EDITORS

Have You Ever Wondered If You Could Write A Harlequin Novel?

Here's great news—Harlequin is offering a series of cassette tapes to help you do just that. Written by Harlequin editors, these tapes give practical advice on how to make your characters—and your story—come alive. There's a tape for each contemporary romance series Harlequin publishes.

Mail order only

All sales final
